MW00898969

DAMNED IF I KNOW

RALPH WEDGEWORTH

DAMNED IF I KNOW

This is a work of fiction. All the characters, names, incidents, organizations, and dialogue in this novel are either the products of the author's imagination or are used fictitiously.

iUniverse books may be ordered through booksellers or by contacting:

iUniverse
1663 Liberty Drive
Bloomington, IN 47403
www.iuniverse.com
1-800-Authors (1-800-288-4677)

ISBN: 978-1-5320-6597-2 (sc)
ISBN: 978-1-5320-6598-9 (e)

Library of Congress Control Number: 2019901763

Print information available on the last page.

iUniverse rev. date: 03/14/2019

ACKNOWLEDGMENTS

I would like to thank the members of the Writer's Bloc for their support. Bill Defries, Anson Cadogan, David Wright, Stephan Macintaya—these talented individuals helped to make this project possible.

A special thanks goes to two people who were instrumental in the completion of the novel: C. C. Alexander, who read the book back to me time and time again as we traveled, and Suzanne Wesson, who helped to get the manuscript from handwritten to typed format.

1

Even though the monitor for her desktop was lit up top to bottom with images and data of current cases, Kat Gonzales looked at the screen as though it was blank. Her focus was four miles away in an old abandoned warehouse on the west side of Corpus Christi. She looked at her watch. *Damn*, she thought. In less than ten minutes, the culmination of her work over the past eleven months would come to a head.

"I gotta get out of here," Kat said to no one in particular as she headed for the elevator. Nobody bothered to ask why she was leaving or to say bye. "Typical," she said as she pushed the Down button. As the door opened, Kat was greeted with a familiar face.

Carlos Vera smiled. "Hey, I was just on my way up to see you. Where you headed?"

"Where d'you think?"

"Want some company?"

"What you drivin'?" Kat asked.

"On a cop's salary? What do you think?"

"The Bronco? That's perfect. Let's roll."

The brisk November wind swirled around Kat as she exited the police station and walked across the parking lot. She peered out over the bay. *Damn*, she thought, *a view like this and only one fuckin' window in the building.*

Once inside the vehicle, as they were buckling up, Carlos asked, "Are you sure Captain Salinas is down with this?"

"What Captain Salinas doesn't know—which is a lot, I might add—won't hurt him. Drive."

Carlos headed west, crossing uptown Corpus, taking directions from Kat.

"Pull over there, across from that Buick. I want to be able to see without being seen."

They watched as SWAT entered the warehouse. Kat and Carlos listened intently for gunfire but heard none.

"That's a good sign," Carlos said.

Kat shook her head. "What if nobody is in there? What if my intel was bad? All that time I put in, being around those thugs. I can hear it now, back at the sta—" She broke off abruptly and pointed to the transport vans that were arriving. Patrol officers began the process of determining which gang members would be carted off in which van.

Kat counted at least thirty in handcuffs. A few looked like teenagers, but most were older. Kat had been up close and personal with several of the leaders. "There—that's Arrow. That motherfucker threatened my life."

"I see Frog and that pissant Hector. Way to go, Kat. Those guys will be away for a long time."

A familiar vehicle pulled up alongside the Bronco. "Figured you might be here. Nice work." And with that, Captain Salinas drove on past them.

"Nice work," Kat thought. *That's pretty much all I needed to hear.* Those two words made all the time and effort she had put into organizing this bust worthwhile. Kat could go to Pepe's Tavern now and drink all the Dos Equis she wanted without having to buy a single beer; her cop buddies would see to that.

Things were a lot different now, a lot better. She had struggled the first few years after being promoted from Vice to a unit specializing in Narcotics. The good old boys hadn't exactly welcomed her with open arms. Nobody even spoke to her for the first few weeks after the transfer. She'd had the same thought nearly every day as she left work: *To hell with these assholes. They don't know who they are messing with. I'll show them.*

In Vice, she was special. She had been recruited shortly after graduating from the police academy. She was young and naive enough to think her abilities had been recognized and that she was on the fast track to the top. In reality, they only wanted her in Vice because of her appearance; they wanted to use her in their prostitution stings. At five foot seven and close to 135 pounds, she was just what they needed. She had been an athlete in high school—a runner. Now, she was still fit and trim, but she had curves in all the right places. Numerous women who had asked her who had done her boob job were disappointed when Kat had replied, "Mother Nature, of course." She wore her jet-black hair down when off duty. The tips reached just below her shoulder blades. Her eyes were as dark as her hair. Her nickname in junior high had been Pocahontas because she could have passed as a Native American. Kat didn't mind the reference; her father's grandmother had been Cherokee. Kat was proud of her Native American heritage but prouder still of her Hispanic origins, even when others seemed to not be.

Initially, the men in Vice fell over themselves trying to be nice to her. Once she busted their balls a time or two, they all backed off and acted like she was one of the boys.

That was exactly what she wanted—just to be one of the boys.

Kat, born Katarina Gonzales, had four older brothers who picked on her constantly. She hated it when she was growing up but came to appreciate just how tough that had made her once she entered high school. Nobody messed with Kat, not even the guys. She was so pretty that most of the boys her age were afraid to ask her out. That didn't matter. Seniors took her on dates her freshman year, and she went out with college boys for the next three years of high school. Oh, those college boys—they did things high school boys only dreamed about. Besides, there weren't any good-looking high school boys in Alice, Texas, anyway.

Shortly after graduation, Kat attended a community college in nearby Corpus Christi. She wanted to become a teacher but fell in love with the professor in one of her elective classes. The next semester, Kat took every class that professor taught. He was in his midthirties, slender, with deep blue eyes that seemed to look right into her core. She had to practically throw herself at him before he finally asked her to meet him at a bar just outside of town. He was married but wasn't living with his wife, who was living out of state. None of that mattered to Kat. This was the first man in her life who hadn't stumbled all over himself trying to get into her pants. He was the coolest, and Kat wanted him to want her.

Thinking back now, she realized that SOB had used her. She still couldn't believe she had paid for the hotel room that night. He'd told her that he couldn't have a hotel bill showing up on his credit card statements. The sex was good but not great. He was more into pleasuring himself, and Kat was not used to that. She soon realized that the professor was not all that she had made him out to be. She still finished his classes and got her As, but the professor was not back on campus the next semester. Rumor was that he'd been caught with a dean's wife and his leave of absence was actually a cover for his ass getting fired.

Although she'd taken the classes to be near the professor, Kat actually liked the subject matter—criminal justice. She finished her two-year degree, and upon graduating at the top of her class, she applied to the thirteen-week academy for the Corpus Christi Police Department. Corpus was on the water, and running down the bay front along Ocean Drive as part of their conditioning made her want to do it all the more. The weeks flew by, and once again Kat received top honors at graduation. She was now a police officer, a cop.

Being a cop, however, was not as special as Kat had envisioned. The hours were long, and she got little or no respect from the people she stopped while patrolling in her police cruiser. The women were pissed that it wasn't a male cop who had stopped them. It was as if they thought they might get out of a ticket if they turned on the charm. Even the ugly bitches seemed disappointed. The male drivers were even worse, especially the Hispanic ones. They were not about to appear subordinate to a female, cop or no cop.

Her fellow officers weren't much better. Kat had expected that; they gave all the rookies a tough time. But it seemed to Kat that she received a little extra when it came to shittin' on the new guy. Kat was paired with a seasoned officer to help with her on-the-job training. He embarrassed her when he told the other police officers that she'd fallen down while getting out of the car on her first traffic stop. He was such an ass to Kat that after she'd had her fill, she fired back, while in the presence of several other officers, "If you aren't in my panties, then don't be riding my ass." She couldn't believe she'd said it, but it did the trick. He never tried to make her look bad again. He was all business, no nonsense there, and she appreciated that.

It wasn't a difficult decision when Vice came calling. "Let's see—stay here in patrol and continue to be treated like crap or go to where my skills can be appreciated. I'll have to think about that." (She did—for all of about fifteen seconds.) She didn't tell them yes right then and there, but she could have. She asked for a couple of days to consider the offer and left it at that. She didn't want to seem too eager.

Kat thrived in Vice. It seemed to be second nature to her. At first they had her positioned on a corner of Leopard Street, waiting on johns to proposition her. Leopard started in the center of downtown Corpus Christi, but the farther from town you went, the wilder it became. It was too easy at first; then word must have spread about her, and her busts were few and far between. She moved to the club scene and started busting the dealers who hung out in the nightclubs. It didn't take long for her reputation to precede her into every dive in Corpus. Next, they tried the internet scene. Her picture on Craigslist drew in dozens of hits a day. She was getting calls from all walks of life. The busts were steady, but it just seemed to Kat that there was more for her to offer than arresting lowlifes looking to score a piece of ass.

She convinced her captain to allow her to focus on the drugs brought in and sold by the major gangs in Corpus Christi. She quickly learned the ins and outs and the who's who in the Corpus gangs. The cool part about it was that Kat could go undercover for days, sometimes even weeks, to get into the workings of some of the gangs.

The 412s were wannabes. They were into their rides, and everything else was just a front to make them appear badder than what they were. They stole whatever they could easily acquire and tagged buildings in their area, but that was just to help mark their territory. They took their name from the last three digits of the ZIP code where they lived. With the exception of a member called Leon, they were all crappy with a spray can. Consequently, Leon was a busy guy. He had to represent the gang in a professional manner. The 412s did not want to look like posers.

Leon was quite an artist. His masterpieces were just about everywhere. The graffiti patrol was grateful when Kat gave him up to the police. They put that little bastard away, and the graffiti in the 412s' turf dropped to nearly nothing. They soon recruited some junior high shits they had caught tagging in their territory. The little farts were good—not as good as Leon but good enough.

Kat had already proven herself valuable in one regard, but she wanted to go deeper. She wanted to "take a bite out of crime," as she remembered the animated McGruff the Crime Dog say in her childhood days. She wanted to make a difference. She recalled how many of her high school friends in Alice had turned out to be potheads and all-around losers, all because of drugs. She knew she couldn't stop it all, but she could stop some of it.

So Kat left the 412s behind and moved on to bigger and badder things. She started hanging out at the places the Mamba Kings frequented. It wasn't long before she was being hit on by some of the MKs. As the new chick, she thoroughly pissed off the skank bitches the MKs always had in tow. Kat quickly realized that these *rucas* were going to be a bigger problem than the

MKs themselves. She solved both issues by making her move on Rico, the leader of the MKs. Rico liked the attention from the hot chick, and he took her to be his own—and the others knew not to fuck with Kat.

That move saved her ass, and Kat was exactly where she needed to be to get the intel she so desperately wanted. Rico didn't share anything of importance in the beginning, but it wasn't too long before Kat was going with Rico on some of his meets, probably because Rico didn't want any of the other MKs trying to make time with his woman while he was doing business. Kat remembered every detail and every name of the contacts Rico met. She soon had their entire operation mapped out. She could have taken them down at any time, but the MKs were only one gang. Why grab only one beer when you can easily take the whole case? Kat wanted to draw in the La Razas as well. She started planting seeds in Rico's head, telling him he could organize the whole city, and all the other gangs would come to him whenever they wanted to take action against another gang. Hell, he would be the fuckin' Godfather. The Don of Corpus Christi. He admitted that title had a nice ring to it, even though he had never seen the movie; he'd seen *Scarface*, though, and that was close enough.

Rico sent out feelers to the 412s and the La Razas. The 412s jumped at the chance. It was their proof that they were a legitimate force to be reckoned with. The La Razas were not so quick to join in. They had been around for thirty years in Corpus and were doing fine all by themselves. They didn't need—and didn't want—to be associated with another gang, especially the 412s.

Kat had her work cut out for her, trying to get the La Razas on board. Rico said none of this would work without the cooperation of the La Razas. She went about it carefully, but she managed to make Rico think *he* had come up with the idea for Kat to befriend some of the La Razas and eventually get them to see how they would benefit. She and Rico agreed it would take a long time for this to occur. They said their goodbyes and promised each other that they would get back together, once the plan was in place.

It could not have ended any better for Kat.

Once again Kat found herself in a dive where another gang was known to hang out. She had more experience this time around and managed to stay on the fringe of the gang, thus not alerting the suspicions of the gang members; better yet, the bitches left her alone. She received intelligence on the La Razas from the gang task force, thus cutting down on the amount of time it would take to infiltrate them. She selected a few of the second-level gang members and waited for an opportunity to present itself.

It took several weeks, but finally two of the La Razas she had chosen came into Chewey's, a roach-infested dump that said it was a restaurant on the sign outside, but no one she saw ever ate the food there. It was all about the cervezas, shooting pool, and the drugs. Two La Razas—Hector and Frog—came in without the company of anyone else. Kat knew this was her chance. She ordered her Dos Equis dressed with lime and salt, walked over to the pool table where the boys were about halfway through a game, and placed her quarters on the edge.

"This game is closed, sista," said Hector.

"I can take the both of you," Kat retorted. "We'll play for a cerveza for starters and see how it goes from there. You boys chicken?"

Frog scowled. "It'll cost you more than a beer to get into this game, *chica*."

Kat realized she had piqued Frog's interest, at least; the verdict was still out on Hector. Kat reasoned that if she could win Frog over, Hector would soon follow. "What did ya have in mind?" she asked.

"We beat your ass; you give up that ass," said Frog.

"That sounds fair," Hector said.

"What's in it for me if I win?" she asked.

Hector laughed. "If you win, you get to choose which one of us you want to fuck first."

He's definitely on board now, Kat thought. "How can I possibly pass up a chance like that?" she said coyly. "But I have a better idea. Let's play for cervezas right now. I need to get a little drunk before I go ballin' someone in the bathroom."

Cutthroat was the game. Each player had five balls, and the object of the game was to knock in the balls of the other two players. Kat had balls 1 through 5. Frog chose 6 through 10. That left 11 through 15 for Hector. When all five of one player's balls were made, that player would have to buy beers for the remaining players. Kat was an expert at pool—she could have easily knocked Hector out right after the break—but she let them win the first game. *My brothers would be proud of me*, she thought, *or would they?*

Kat thought about her brothers taking her to Rusty's Pool Hall when she was just ten years old. They were supposed to be taking her to the Alice city swimming pool. "Hey," they'd told her, "this is pool. Quit your bitchin' and grab a cue." They must have let her win because she never complained once after that first time. She didn't really like wearing her bathing suit to the pool hall, but her brothers said that their mom would know something was up if she didn't.

Kat bought the beers and put the quarters in for the next game. This time she knocked Hector out before she let Frog win. While Hector was getting the beers, Kat asked, "How did you get a name like Frog?"

Hector overheard and laughed. "He bit the head off a frog."

Kat's mouth dropped open. "Was it already dead?"

"Naw, man. The legs were still kicking. It was fuckin' wild. It freaked out some of the bitches. Celeste threw up. That bitch was weird anyway."

Frog didn't say anything; he just grinned.

"Why in hell would you do such a thing to a poor little ole frog?" asked Kat.

"No reason. At the time I thought it would be cool. I was thirteen years old. I was fuckin' stupid. Now, no one knows my real name. Everyone just calls me Frog."

"What *is* your real name?"

"Cesar," he said. "Cesar Talamontez. And you?"

"I'm Kat … Katherine Barrera," she lied smoothly. She didn't need any sick retaliation from the La Razas, once she made the bust, if they knew her real name.

Hector returned with the beers. "Hey, we gonna fuck or not?"

Kat shrugged. "It's still too early to tell. Put your quarters in, and rack 'em."

Kat carefully hid her pool skills, and two games turned into ten. Both boys seemed more than a little drunk and more than a little horny. Kat knew she had to make her exit before things got out of hand, but she needed to keep her new friends happy. These boys would be her way in to the La Razas. "Listen, fellas, I'd love nothing more than to spend the rest of the day with you guys, but I gotta get going. Rain check on the fuckin', okay?"

"You can't go. You can't lead us on like that and just walk out. No fuckin' way, bitch," Hector growled.

"Well, baby, I will be back," Kat said. "What about you? You got some other bitch who can kick your ass in pool like I can? Tell you what—same place, same time tomorrow?"

"Definitely," said Frog.

"Yeah, we'll be here," Hector agreed.

"Okay, then, I'll see you boys tomorrow. Bring your quarters."

Kat felt relief settle in with each breath she took as she stepped outside Chewey's. She wasn't sure she could make it to her car before collapsing from the stress of her performance. Once inside her red Mustang, she sat motionless behind the steering wheel. "Get a grip lady," Kat said aloud. "You have to be able to do this. Otherwise, the whole plan goes to shit." She took a deep breath. "You can do it," she reassured herself. "You can do this."

Feeling more confident now, Kat drove to her apartment on the south side of town. Once there, she called her dad. She always had called him whenever she got rattled, whether it was due to sports, school, or assholes from work. Dad seemed to always know what to say to help her get her head back together. She knew, though, that she couldn't tell him the details of what had happened—not for any security reasons but because he was her dad.

I can just hear his reaction if I were to say, "Hey, Dad, I just played two gangbangers for beers and a piece of my ass." Yeah, that would go over real well. Nope, she couldn't tell him anything about it, but she wanted to hear his voice. She just wanted him to make it all better.

"Hey, Dad, what ya doing?"

"Not much. Just watchin' the Braves kick the crap out of the Astros. What's up with you, *mija*?"

Kat knew her dad cussed all the time, but he was always careful not to let it slip in front of her, and she appreciated that. He loved her and respected her as well. Nothing but the best for his baby girl.

"I'm just in the middle of a big case. I've been working on it for several months, and it's just hard right now. No big deal, though. How are you and Mom doing?"

"Your mom and I are fine. No need to worry about us. Anything I can do to help you out with your case? Need me to come down there to that police station and kick some butts?"

Kat giggled. "No, Daddy. No one down there needs their butts kicked. I just wanted to call and tell you I love you, and I miss you."

"Well, you can tell me and your mom in person tomorrow night—dinner, seven o'clock. I'll tell your mom to pick up some of that suzi crap you like so much."

"It's sushi, Dad. No, sorry, I can't make it tomorrow. Tied up with work and all, but thanks anyway. Next time."

"Okay, but Sunday your mom's cooking menudo. See you around one o'clock, unless you want to come early and go to mass with us. Everyone would love to see you. Ain't been to communion over here in a couple of months now. They all been asking about you."

"I'll think about it. Thanks, Dad. See you guys Sunday."

It didn't take much for Kat to feel grounded again. *Good old Dad. Okay, now back to work. How can I get those two clowns to get me in with the La Razas?*

After talking with her dad, Kat's next call went to Carlos Vera, a fellow police officer who graduated from the academy with her. He'd showed great promise, and Kat now felt he could help with her situation. Carlos was more than happy to lend a hand.

"It just so happens I'm off tomorrow," he told her. "I can meet you at Chewey's."

Carlos arrived at the dive a little before one o'clock that afternoon. Except for the bartender and the walking advertisement for Valtrex that served as a waitress, Carlos had the place to himself. He ordered a Corona, dressed, and put some quarters into one of the pool tables in the back. He wanted to be near the action so Kat could easily drag him in. He hadn't played pool in years, and it showed, but Kat had told him it would be better if he sucked at pool.

Around one thirty, two guys came strolling into the place like they belonged there. Carlos figured them to be Frog and Hector. They glared at Carlos and went straight to the bar. "See, motherfucker? I told you that bitch wouldn't be here," Hector said.

"She'll be here," Frog said confidently. "She'll be here."

The La Razas took the table two down from Carlos and started playing, but Carlos could tell they were keeping an eye on him. *Trying to figure out why this motherfucker is here, huh?* Carlos thought. *Damn, I hope Kat gets here soon.*

As if on cue, Kat strolled into Chewey's, acting as if she didn't have a care in the world. She smiled at the La Razas and said, "So you boys back for another ass-whippin' like the one I gave y'all yesterday? I hope you brought your quarters for the table and your dollars for the cervezas. You're gonna need a lot of both. I'm feelin' real lucky today."

"What makes you think we even want to play yo' ass today? You walked out on us yesterday," said Hector.

Kat shrugged. "Well, if you're too scared ..."

"Nobody's scared," said Frog "Rack 'em up."

"I won yesterday, remember? You rack 'em." Kat headed to the bar, leaving the boys to ponder her ass as she walked away. She had a good ass and knew they were checking it out. A quick glimpse in the cracked and dusty mirror behind the bar confirmed it. She came back with a dressed Dos Equis and said, "I don't know why I bought this beer. I should've just waited for the first game to be over, but Hector is slow as shit with the rack. I was afraid I'd die of thirst before the break."

Hector placed the last ball into the rack. "Fuck you. Same as yesterday? Cutthroat?"

Kat shook her head, "No, let's play 8 ball. Cutthroat is too boring."

"We can't play 8 ball with three people," chided Hector.

Kat pointed to Carlos. "Ask that guy. We can play partners."

"He's your partner, then," Frog said, "'cause he damn sure ain't gonna be mine."

"Mine neither; he sucks," said Hector.

"Okay, he can be my partner, and we will still kick your ass," said Kat as she walked over to ask the new guy to play.

"No, no, I haven't played in a while. I'm not very good. I would just mess up your game. Trust me; find somebody else," said Carlos.

Kat looked around the bar. "Where we gonna find somebody else? Get yourself over here, and let's play pool."

Carlos walked over and extended his hand to Hector and Frog. They ignored him and took a swig of their beers.

"I'm Kat, and these two assholes are Frog and Hector. You don't want to shake their hands anyway. No tellin' where they've been." Kat laughed. "And who might you be?"

"I'm Carlos."

"What brings you to Chewey's?" Hector asked.

"Just bored. I'm in town on business. I used to come in here a lot when I lived in Corpus. This place has changed."

"What kinda business you in?" Hector asked.

"Sales."

"What kinda sales?" Hector asked.

"Pharmaceuticals."

Both Hector and Frog burst out laughing. "You a drug pusher?" Frog asked.

"No, nothing like that. Everything I sell is prescription."

"A prescription drug pusher," Frog said. "That sounds interesting. How 'bout we play some pool, and we can talk about this prescription drug pushin' as we go?"

Hector broke and made the 2 ball in the corner pocket. "Solids. We be solids, homey." He missed an easy shot on the 1 ball in the side pocket.

"Gonna make this easy for us, huh?" Kat said as she proceeded to make five striped balls in a row. She was about to run the table but thought better of it. She missed her next shot, a bank shot into the side pocket.

Frog took over and made three balls before he tried to run the 6 ball down the rail. Carlos gave it his best effort but was unable to make the 10 ball in the corner pocket, although he did manage to knock in one of the solids as he missed.

Damn, either Carlos is really good, or he's the worst pool player I've seen in a long time, Kat thought as she saw the wrong ball fall into the pocket.

"All even," Hector said as he walked around the table, scoping out his next shot. "How 'bout we up the ante? We lose; we buy shots and beers. You lose; pusher-man here goes to his car and brings back some samples."

"No way," said Carlos. "I could get fired. They take that shit very serious. I agreed to play for a beer, and that's all."

"You mean you got some badass shit just sittin' in your car? Why the fuck we still playing pool?" asked Frog. "Let's go get some dope, pusher-man, and I'll *buy* you a beer." Frog laughed.

"Hey, lay off," Kat intervened. "We can play pool for now, and if Carlos does have some samples in his car, maybe he can share when we're done. That sound cool to everyone?"

"Sure, beer now; drugs later. Sounds like my kinda day," said Hector as he lined up his next shot. He made the two remaining solids but missed making the 8 ball. Kat could have easily made the last two striped balls but missed on her first shot.

Frog knocked the 8 in the corner. "Modelo," Frog said smugly. "Don't want none of that American crap beer."

Kat walked to the bar to get the beers. Carlos shoved his quarters into the table and started racking the balls for the next game.

Three games later, the boys were out of patience; they wanted some of Carlos's samples.

"It's time, compadre," said Frog.

"Yep, we been playin' long enough. Time for something a little stronger than cervezas," Hector said.

"No can do, friend," answered Carlos. "Everything is inventoried. I can't just go hand out controlled substances to anyone. Maybe I don't even like you guys."

Hector bristled. "Maybe we smash yo' face, motherfucker. 'I don't like you guys.'"

Kat stepped in between the men with arms outstretched to keep them apart. "Wait, wait, wait. We can all work this out without anyone getting their motherfuckin' face smashed in. Just give me a minute with Carlos, okay?"

"Fine," said Frog. "Just don't plan to leave Chewey's without handing over some samples."

Kat and Carlos sat down at a table well away from Hector and Frog.

"What are we gonna do? I don't have any drugs in my car," said Carlos.

"Got it covered," Kat said. "Captain gave me two bottles of oxycodone to make this shit happen. I will follow you to your car. You open the trunk and act like you're handing them to me. I'll take it from there."

"I'm not leaving you alone with those two fuckers. No telling what they might do to you once I'm gone."

Kat stood firm, "This is what we talked about. This is how it must go down. Don't worry about me. I can handle these two. It's the next step that has me concerned."

"Okay, I don't like it one bit, but we'll play it like you said. Only one thing—I'll drive around the corner and wait for an all-clear text from you. I'll give you ten minutes. If I don't get a text stating everything's cool, I'll return with backup. Clear?"

"Better make it twenty minutes," Kat said. "I don't want to blow this. I've put in way too much time, and we're *this close*"—Kat put her index finger within an inch of her thumb—"to nailing their asses."

"Fine. You got twenty minutes. Not one second more."

"Cool. Let me go set this up with da boys over there."

Kat left Carlos at the table and walked over to Frog and Hector, who were still playing pool but watching Kat and Carlos.

"Our friend there is a little nervous around you two," she said.

"Well, he better be," said Hector. "I can't wait to bust a cap in his ass. 'Our friend,' my ass."

"So what's the deal?" Frog asked coolly.

"He said he has a bottle for each of you and that he can get more—lots more. He wants to know if you guys can sell it and split the money with him. He's talking like maybe a thousand dollars a week at first, and if all goes well, it could be closer to twenty grand a month."

Frog narrowed his eyes. "What's the catch?"

"No catch," said Kat. "He gets the stuff, you guys unload it on the street, and everyone walks away with some paper in their pockets. Can't get much easier than that."

"You have our attention," said Frog. "How do we go about getting the stuff?"

"That's where I come in," said Kat. "He doesn't trust you guys. He'll give me the stuff on Sunday, and I'll make the transfer the same day. You guys do whatever you do and give me the money, plus 5 percent for my commission, on Saturday. Sound fair?"

"Five percent, huh? For what?" asked Hector.

"I take five from you guys and five from him, and I make this whole thing happen. Otherwise, I walk over to the Mamba Kings, and I bet they jump at the chance."

"Hold on, hold on," said Frog. "Nobody's walking nowhere."

"So, is that a yes? You boys wanna get rich or what?"

"Yep," Hector said. "Now what about the samples?"

"Look, I'm gonna walk him to his car, get the stuff, and meet you back here. We can work out the details then. He wants to get the hell out of here."

"You two ain't going out of here alone," Hector said. "You take off, and we don't get shit."

"You're not listening. He doesn't want to deal directly with you. That's where I come in, okay? There needs to be some level of trust here. We all have a shitload of money riding on this."

"Okay, cool," Frog said. "Don't make us wait. I don't like to wait."

"Be right back." Kat stood up and headed over to meet Carlos at the door.

"Everything cool?" asked Carlos.

Kat nodded. "We're cool. Let's get going."

The two of them walked to Carlos's Ford Bronco. Carlos used his remote to pop the back lid over the tailgate. He pretended to put something into

Kat's purse; he assumed the two men were watching. "Remember—twenty minutes," Carlos said. "And then I come running."

"Gotcha. And thanks. You were perfect. I couldn't have done it without you."

Carlos closed the tailgate and lid, got into his Bronco and drove around the corner, and parked. Kat turned and walked back to Chewey's. Frog and Hector were watching and waiting, just like she expected.

"You boys happy to see me."

"Yeah, we are. We need to work out the deal, though," said Frog. "I called Arrow while you were gettin' the shit."

"Who's Arrow?" Kat asked, although she already knew.

"He's OM—original member. He said to text if you came through with the junk."

"Well, I'm here. Give him a call."

"Where's the stuff?" asked Hector.

"Right here." Kat pulled the two small bottles of oxycodone from her purse and shoved them into Hector's hand. "Enjoy."

"I will." Hector clutched the bottles and went to the back of the bar.

Frog started texting without saying another word.

"Callin' your lover?" Kat asked with a grin.

"No, I'm letting Arrow know you came back with the shit. He wants us to work out the details. He wants to meet with me after we're done. He said that nothing is going to happen unless he gives the okay."

"Tell him that I don't negotiate with the help. I talk to the big dog, or I walk and take the supplier with me. He trusts me. He really doesn't care who sells the shit. I bet the Mamba Kings won't be as difficult."

"Arrow is not gonna like this."

"I don't give a shit what Arrow likes or dislikes. I'm telling you how it's going to be, so *deal with it*."

Frog started dialing as he walked out the back door of Chewey's.

Kat's stomach was in her throat. *Did I play it too rough?* she wondered. *Will they pass on the deal? Back to square one.*

Frog came back from the alley a few minutes later. "Arrow is coming, but he ain't happy 'bout it."

A jolt of adrenaline pulsed through Kat's body. "Great. Let's grab a cerveza and wait. How long you think?"

"Ten, fifteen minutes. He ain't far, but he's busy at the moment."

"Where's Hector?"

"He took off with that shit. He's got a bitch that lives close. I'll never see any of it," answered Frog.

It wasn't long before Arrow and three other La Razas came strolling into Chewey's through the back door. They surprised Kat, who had positioned herself so she could watch for them coming in the front.

Arrow was tall, about six foot four. His top front teeth were silver, and the bottom two were capped in gold. "So this is our little chica that's going to make everybody rich, huh?" Arrow said in a low, deep voice as he slid into the booth beside Frog.

Kat extended her hand to him across the table. "Hi, I'm Kat."

Arrow didn't move. He waited as Kat slowly pulled back her hand. "I know who you are, Kitty Kat. What I want to know is why you got mixed up in this. What you got to prove? You wanna run with the gangstas? Is that it, Kitty Kat? You wanna be one of the bad boys?"

"I just want to make some money, lots of money. I don't know much about you guys. It just worked out this way. I was playing pool with Frog and Hector, and we asked this guy to join us. I didn't know he sold pharmaceuticals. It just came out in conversation."

"It just came out in conversation," Arrow repeated. "How does something like that 'just come out in conversation'?"

Frog jumped in. "Hector and I were just bullshittin' with that *vato* when he said he had samples in his car."

"And where is Hector?" asked Arrow.

"He took off with the samples. Probably went to get fucked up with Fat Sheila," Frog answered.

Kat started again. "I think he came down here looking for someone to sell the drugs for him. We just happened to be in the right spot at the right time. He wants to keep his hands clean and let us do the dirty work."

"By 'us,' you mean the La Razas, not you personally," Arrow said.

"Hey, look, I'm taking a risk here too, you know," Kat said more forcefully. "If you go down, I go down. If he gets caught, I get caught. I've got a lot to lose."

"More than you know, chica; more than you know," Arrow said. "If this goes bad, we will find you. There won't be enough left of your ass to make a taco once we get finished with you. *Comprende*?"

"Yes," Kat answered. "I understand."

"Okay, now to business," Arrow said as though no death threat had occurred. "As I understand it, you get the shipment on Sunday from our little vato and bring it to us. We dispose of the goods and pay you on Saturday. Then we do it all over again the next day. Why pay on Saturday? Why not just do it on Sunday when we get the next shipment?"

Kat shook her head. "I'm not sure. Maybe he wants to make a Saturday deposit. Maybe he wants to make sure he gets paid before he gives you another shipment. He didn't tell me, and I didn't ask. That's just how he wants it to be, okay?"

"I can see that," Frog said.

Arrow glared at Frog. "Don't need your two cents." He turned back to Kat. "We meet on the island, Bob Hall pier, two o'clock Sunday. You know where that is?" He didn't wait for Kat to answer. "Place the stuff in a large ice chest, and put it in the trunk. Leave your door unlocked with the keys hidden under your floor mat. Walk a mile down the beach before you come back. We'll get the ice chest and leave the keys. The beach is wide open, and we'll have eyes everywhere. If you set us up, you won't make it back to Corpus. That's on the reals, chica."

"Okay, I got that part. What about the money drop?" Kat asked.

"Simple. You come here Saturday, same time—two o'clock—and Hector and Frog will have a bag for you."

"Doesn't get any easier than that," Kat said. "Oh, wait—what if something happens? What if he runs into trouble and has to delay the delivery? How do I let you guys know?"

"Text Frog. You two swap numbers before we leave. Frog knows how to find me." Arrow slid out of the booth and walked out the back door, with the three La Razas in tow.

He didn't say goodbye, adios, eat shit and die motherfucker, or anything, Kat thought. "Nice guy, huh?" she said to Frog.

"Not at all. You don't want to fuck with him. He's not lying about killing you. He's done it before. Don't fuck this up. Now give me your number."

Kat had been issued a department phone. She plugged Frog's number into it, said goodbye, and left. *Enough drama for one day,* she thought. *Maybe Mom had some menudo left.* She was going to find out.

Kat waited until Friday to call Frog. She wanted them to be licking their lips in anticipation before she burst their bubble.

"It seems that there might be a problem with getting that much of a prescription drug going to the same location," she told him. "The supplier needs to use several different pharmacies scattered throughout the city. They need to be a mom-and-pop shop, not a chain, like CVS or Walgreen's. He said it'll still work out, but he has to appear to be selling to legitimate pharmacies. Oh, he also said that he could start with much bigger shipments once he gets the info on the pharmacies. Can you let Arrow know? He said it will take a couple of months to get all the locations mapped out. Not to worry, though. Wait—I have a thought. How about you guys start checking out the city to help locate these mom-and-pop pharmacies? I'll do the same. Maybe we won't have to wait that long to get started. I need the money now."

"I'll contact Arrow and get back with you," Frog said.

All there was to do now was wait for the La Razas to take the bait. Everything was working out as planned.

Frog called Kat only fifteen minutes later. "Arrow was really pissed. He wanted to call the whole thing off. He was gonna send some of the other guys after you two. I finally talked him down. I told him everything was still on the table, but that it would just take a little longer. I told him we could use the guys to speed up everything. He's called a meeting to organize the search. We're gonna check out the Yellow Pages and have groups drive around town, checking for locations to use. So you're welcome."

"Well, thanks, I guess," Kat said. "No, really, nice work. I'll get online and start checking things out right now."

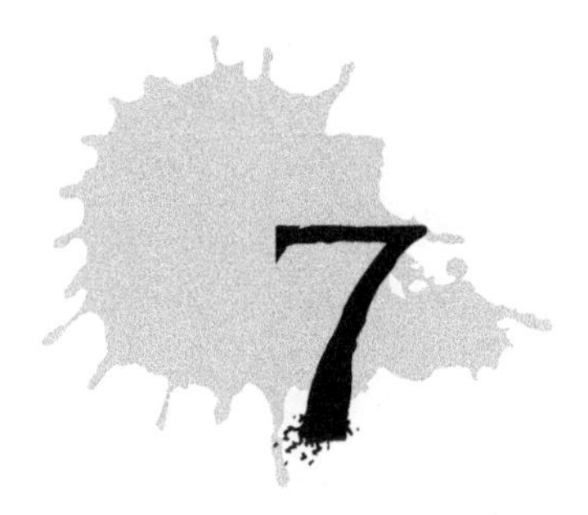

7

Two days passed before Kat gave Frog another ring. "How's the search going?" asked Kat.

"It ain't. We didn't find a single pharmacy."

Kat acted like she couldn't believe her ears, "What? Not even one? Where did you guys look?"

"We stayed in our territory. We looked from Horne to Molina. No luck."

"Well, there's your problem. You didn't go far enough. I found a dozen pharmacies online that we can use. Let's meet, and I'll give you the list."

"Now?"

"Yes, now. You got something more important do?" Kat snapped.

"Okay, see you at Chewey's in twenty."

Frog and Hector were waiting when Kat got to Chewey's. She sat down in the booth next to Frog. Kat didn't care too much for Hector. *Frog has something going on upstairs*, she thought, *but Hector is just a nail waiting on the hammer to fall.*

She pulled the list out of her purse and laid it on the table for both men to see. She didn't like Hector, but she knew better than to show him any disrespect—not yet anyway.

They started shaking their heads as they went down the list, looking at the street addresses of the dozen or so pharmacies Kat had on the list.

"These aren't anywhere near here," Frog said.

"Yeah," Hector agreed, pointing to the list. "These are on the MKs', and those there are on the 412s' turf. We don't do business over there. Not that we're scared or nothin'. We just don't go there, and they don't come over here."

"Well, you guys can either broaden your horizons, or it looks like I take my supplier, and we do business with the MKs and the 412s, whoever they are. I'd hate to leave you boys out of the money—I really like you—but business is business. Talk to Arrow, and see if you can work out some type of deal with the other two gangs. There's enough money in this to make everyone rich."

Kat could tell the wheels were turning in Frog's head. She wasn't sure about Hector. He was so macho that he might just want to pass on the deal. Good thing Frog took the lead.

"Hey, maybe. We ain't never done nothin' like that before, but this is a lot of money. Arrow won't let it go to the MKs or the 412s. I'll tell you that right now."

"Well …" Kat said in her usual drawn-out way, "maybe if it's his idea, Arrow can run the show and just use the MKs and the 412s to get rich. He could cut them in at a lower rate and nobody's to know the difference. Hell, he might even make more money since he would have more punks dealing. It's worth a shot, don't you think?"

Frog nodded. "Yep, that just might work. I'll talk it over with Arrow right now."

"Great. Get back with me on what he says, okay?"

"All right. I'll call either way. Even if he doesn't want in, I might just take a piece of the action for myself. I mean, for me and Hector."

"Smart move," said Kat as she got up from the booth.

Hector and Frog exited through the back door as Kat left from the front. She felt like doing a Tiger Woods' fist pump but suppressed the urge. There would be plenty of time to gloat, once the bust went down. Next item on the plan was to make sure she found out the time and location where the three gangs would meet. *That shouldn't be too hard*, she thought, *if I can just stay close to Frog.*

8

Two days passed without a call from Frog. He didn't return her calls or texts. Kat was beginning to worry that the three gangs would meet before she could find out when and where. It was time to take another trip down to Chewey's.

She walked in, hoping to find either Frog or Hector playing pool. With the exception of the bartender and the smokestack that also served as a waitress, the place was empty. *How in the hell does this place stay open?* Kat thought. *That's another story. One thing at a time right now. I can follow up on that after the bust.*

The city of Corpus Christi had passed laws prohibiting smoking in public establishments, including bars. The place was so dead, though, that the waitress could have been smoking weed instead of cigarettes, and no one would have known. Kat positioned herself in a booth where she could watch both the front and back doors. Two hours passed without a single person coming in. "Damn!" Kat said with emphasis. Then, "Damn, damn, damn it all to hell!" Kat was wiggling and massaging her legs, trying to get the circulation going so she could leave, when lo and behold, Frog and Hector slipped in through the back door. Kat laughed to herself as she played out in her head her best imitation of Al Pacino: *"Say hello to my little friend."*

Hector saw her first. "Hey, what's up? Whatcha doin' here?"

"Got lonely. Wanted to beat you guys in another game of pool. What's been happening with you boys?"

"Not much," said Frog. Then he grinned. "It's set. It's all set. We are about to do the deal."

"Have you guys already set it up with the other gangs?" she asked, her heart in her throat.

"Tomorrow, around two. The MKs and the 412s are gonna meet us, and from what Arrow says, it's pretty much a done deal," Hector said, as if he had played some important role in the matter.

Now Kat had the *when*, but she also needed the *where*. How could she get that without appearing too interested?

Luckily, Frog didn't want to be upstaged by Hector. "Yeah, the meet goes down in an abandoned warehouse about two blocks from here. It's on Morgan by the old Galvan Music House. You plan on coming?"

"No, no, no, no. You boys go have your fun. I've got other things to do. Maybe see you afterward? I was just on my way out—nail appointment. I was hoping to catch you guys earlier. Sorry." Kat almost sprinted out the door. She waited until her Mustang was out of sight before she picked up her phone to call her captain.

Pepe's was packed. The beer was flowing. Everyone was in a good mood and talking loudly. Even the SWAT guys didn't appear too terribly disappointed that they weren't able to blow anyone away. Most of Kat's friends from Vice and all of her fellow officers in the special Narcotics Unit were there. Nothing like this had ever taken place in Corpus Christi. Sure, there had been lots of raids at locations known to be home to gang members, but nothing near this magnitude. And all without anyone getting hurt. Kat lost count of how many times she heard, "Damn, this calls for a promotion." It started her to thinking, *Damn, this* does *call for a promotion*.

She could hardly wait to read tomorrow's paper. She was certain the *Caller Times* would run it as their lead story. She also wanted to watch all three of the local stations' news program to see how much coverage they would give to her bust. Surely it would be the lead story on all broadcasts. What else could be more important than smashing the life out of three gangs here in town?

Almost everyone was still at Pepe's when six o' clock rolled around. Although there was not a sober individual there, a coordinated hush fell over the place when the news came on the three TV sets positioned around the bar. Each set was tuned to a different channel so everyone involved could once again revel in their glory when all of Corpus found out what a wonderful job they'd done.

But although each station had a different lead story, none of them included the day's bust. It wasn't until the weather came on, with no mention of their brave deeds in the early part of the broadcast, that a huge wave of disappointment spread throughout the bar. Some slammed their mugs down hard, while others began cussing loudly. Most just got up and left, mumbling to each other as they walked to their vehicles. A few officers came by and patted Kat on the back. One said, "It's too soon for them to have the information. It'll be covered on the ten o'clock news."

Kat thanked them for their support, but she wasn't sticking around for four more hours. She was going home, not to her apartment but to her home in Alice. She wanted to be with her family.

10

Albarro Gonzales was an early riser and always had been, even before he joined the military straight out of high school. Kat knew he had already read the paper front to back before she even considered getting out of bed. When Kat finally walked into the kitchen for a cup of coffee, she could see the headlines in the *Caller Times*. There was nothing about her bust. Her dad was making *migas*, her favorite breakfast.

"Did it make the paper?" Kat asked her dad.

"Page two. Didn't say very much about it. Sorry, mija."

Kat turned to page two and read the story. It was only two paragraphs, and there was no mention of her name. *That's actually good*, Kat thought. She didn't want those asshole gangbangers finding out her real name. Corpus was a small enough town that she would likely cross paths with other gang members who hadn't been arrested. She would deal with that if and when it occurred. For now, she wanted a promotion, and she felt the publicity would help increase her chances of getting one. Too bad it wasn't going to be that easy.

The next day Kat had to report back to work. After being undercover for several months, what a let-down that was. Even though it took the bad guys off the streets, Kat couldn't see herself going back to her old job. She needed something more. Homicide—now that's where her talents could best be used. When she checked, though, there weren't any positions available. *I guess I'll just have to bide my time and be ready to pounce if one does come open.*

Kat went to work, filling out forms on her computer and answering questions about the bust from the district attorney's office.

"Let's make sure these guys stay away for a real long time," she said. "I want to be able to focus on my job and not be looking over my shoulder to see who's coming up behind me."

She finished her paperwork and interviews on the bust and then quickly moved on to the next assignment. She wasn't going to give the upper echelon a reason to pass her over when a new position in Homicide finally opened up.

"Most of those guys are old. Maybe one will retire soon," she kept telling herself. "Just do your job and be the very best at it. Your time will come."

12

It took over eight years of exemplary performance, but her time finally came. Kat was going to Homicide. At last, she would be a detective. This news was too good; she had to tell somebody. She could hardly wait to phone her mom and dad.

Kat knew she would be the new girl all over again, but that didn't matter at the moment. She had proven that she could handle herself.

Within the week, Kat reported to Homicide. As expected, her arrival was met coolly by the other officers, all of whom had at least a dozen years more experience on the force than Kat.

"Well, you can't teach an old dog new tricks," her dad had told her. "But a Kat can learn pretty quickly. You go kick some butt, girl."

That she did.

Kat knew better than to offer suggestions during meetings. Nobody wanted a newbie telling them how they should do things. They'd been doing it a certain way for as long as they could remember, and it had worked just fine.

Coming up through the ranks, she'd heard numerous times, "If it ain't broke, don't fix it."

It seemed to Kat that the system was broken. The number of homicide cases had risen from fifteen the previous year to nearly double that this year. And to make matters worse, ten of them appeared to be by the same individual. Corpus Christi had a serial killer on their hands, and the police were no closer to catching the guy than they had been a year ago when the killings appeared to have begun.

Kat put all her energy and extra time into this case. She even went into the station on the weekends and her days off. The guys still treated her with scant respect, but she knew that would change if she could solve this case. This one case could substantially reduce the amount of time it would take for the other detectives to accept her as one of their own.

13

The killer was targeting homeless individuals, mostly males, but there had been at least two female victims. All the victims had been poisoned with isopropyl alcohol, the type used for cleaning wounds. Isopropyl alcohol, Kat knew, was extremely toxic if ingested. It caused blindness, coma, and even death.

Captain Moore, her immediate boss in Homicide, seemed to be a very capable police officer. He was always at the police station, unless he was investigating a scene or appearing in court to give testimony. His success rate in solving homicides was among the highest in the state. He took great pride in this—and in his personal appearance. Kat never once saw him without a name-brand suit on—all custom-fitted, as far as she could tell. She often wondered how he could always look so good when he often worked twelve to fifteen hours a day.

"Captain Robert Moore," he said to Kat as he introduced himself on her first day working for him. "But you can call me Bob. Bob is easy to remember, isn't it? Spelled the same frontward and backward." He seemed so down-to-earth. Everybody liked Bob. Kat did too. He was the only detective who introduced himself that day. The other guys just sat at their desks, working on their computers or answering the phones—clearly ignoring Kat.

Even though Captain Moore was quite a bit older than Kat, she saw him as very attractive, like Richard Gere. His salt-and-pepper hair was cut short and always styled with every hair in place, something nearly impossible to do with the constant winds coming off the bay front in Corpus. The station was located on John Sartain Street, just two blocks off the water. Kat's friend

Claudia would say that because of the humidity and wind, you could wash and dry your hair by just walking across the parking lot to the police station. That was one reason why Kat liked to keep her hair straight.

She knew that Bob was in his early fifties and married. She reasoned that he must not have much of a home life because he was rarely there. He probably dreaded going home. What woman who really loved her man would put up with being alone all the time? *Or maybe she's not always alone*, Kat thought. *Oh well, I'm getting distracted. Time to focus on the case.*

It took a few months before anyone on the police force realized that there had been a substantial increase in the number of deaths in homeless victims. It might have taken even longer, had Father Jimenez not gone to the local media, raising holy hell because the homeless were dying in the streets, and no one was doing anything about it.

It wasn't that the Corpus Christi Police Department didn't care or wasn't doing their job. It was that the victims all appeared to have died of natural causes. They were each found with a bottle of whiskey in their hands or nearby. It was never the same brand of whiskey, but it was always a new bottle. The victims were not confined to just one part of town. The body count stretched from as far south as Flour Bluff and all the way north to Annaville, a distance of about fifteen miles. What made matters worse was that no identification was found on the bodies. This made identifying the victims extremely tough, unless they had been arrested at some point or had been in the military; then their fingerprints could be compared to a database. Other homeless people and the good folks operating the shelters could look at a picture and often give a first name, but last names were hard to recall.

Of course there were never any witnesses to the deaths.

The medical examiner's office was not to blame either. Dr. Dimas Elizondo would come in on Monday morning and survey the number of yellow tags tacked to the bulletin board, indicating the number of bodies that had been brought in since he had left on Friday afternoon. Not all of them would need a complete autopsy. Dr. Elizondo would do a thorough external examination on each cadaver, as well as draw blood from different locations and vitreous fluid from the eye to perform mostly routine tests. Occasionally, the doctor would order a full workup if he suspected something unusual, but that was rarely the case.

Recently, the alcohol levels in the victims were high enough to cause death, so the good doctor had no cause for opening them up for a complete autopsy. The bodies would be rolled back into the cooler, and there they would remain on the plastic tray table until they could be identified and their next of kin notified. Dr. Elizondo had a very efficient staff. Most of the bodies were picked up by a funeral home after the families had been notified. A few, though, had to be buried by the county because they could not be identified, or the family wouldn't pay funeral expenses for a long-lost relative that no one cared about.

Kat reviewed surveillance tapes from local businesses near where each of the bodies had been found. Some of these business had cameras aimed at the areas in front of their stores. She was looking for someone who was in more than one location. Maybe that would be the connection. No such luck. It did get her noticed by some of the other detectives, though.

"How could someone be giving all these people poisoned whiskey," Kat asked aloud in the office, "and no one ever saw it? You can't walk down the street where these bodies have been found without getting hit up for spare change. Surely if someone was handing out whiskey bottles, that would attract attention, don't you think?"

Javier Aguilar, who had made the move to Homicide two years ago, said, "Yeah, but these bums don't want to come forward. Most are wanted by the police somewhere, and they figure if they talk, we'll ask more questions than they want to answer. So they are playing dumb to protect themselves. Stupid assholes. Don't they know we're trying to help? That somebody out there is going around pickling them from the inside out?"

Kat understood Detective Aguilar's point, but there had to be more to it than that. She tried to come up with ways in which a person could pass off bottles of alcohol without being noticed. If someone in a car had just stopped and rolled down a window to hand an unsuspecting victim his last drink, the homeless population would have surrounded the vehicle, hoping for some of the same. Maybe the killer had left bottles at random locations during the day, hoping some unfortunate fellow would stumble by later that night and drink until his lights turned out. Nah, couldn't happen. If it was left in plain sight, then someone would have seen it and drunk it during the day. All the deaths occurred at night.

Maybe someone at one of the shelters was playing God and euthanizing the poor devils. *That would give us motive*, she thought, *but how does he select his victims? And better yet, how does he give them the bottle in the first place? Why is it always a different whiskey? It's not like these people had discriminating tastes.* Kat knew these were all important pieces of the puzzle. All she had to do was put them together to make them fit.

Kat started riding the bus on her nights off. The city had the B-Line, large red buses mostly used by the underprivileged. It had routes that covered the major streets and locations all over Corpus. Lots of college students took the bus from their apartments to the university on a daily basis. What if one of them was the killer? He could easily sit beside one of the indigents and secretly pass him a bottle. The homeless raised enough money by begging on corners at major intersections to afford to ride the bus. How else could they get to some of those locations? It would take them hours to walk. Kat's brain was firing on all cylinders. She was positive that the exchange was taking place on the B. It had routes that went to Flour Bluff and other routes headed to Annaville. She felt she was on to something.

It had been almost a month since the last homeless person had been found poisoned. Time for the killer to make his move. Kat had been riding the bus every night for two weeks. The lack of sleep made her cranky, but if she could catch this guy, it would all be worth it in the end. The B-Line didn't run all night long. Kat felt she had just been along for the ride when a young male, about twenty-five years old, boarded the bus and sat down near a man who obviously hadn't bathed in days and his clothes had not seen a washing machine in weeks. Why would a well-kept young man sit anywhere near this odiferous individual? Everyone else sat as far away as possible.

Kat's pulse quickened. This had to be the killer, but how could she prove it? She couldn't just go up and arrest him for sitting next to a stinking man. She waited until the young man exited the bus, and she ran for the same exit. Kat intentionally tripped on the last step and fell face first onto the man's back, knocking him to the ground. Immediately, Kat was on top of the guy, pulling out her handcuffs before he could even move his arms, which she had pinned next to his body with her legs.

The lady bus driver still had the door open and saw everything. She asked Kat if she was okay.

"Yes, yes, I'm fine. I'm detective Katarina Gonzales with the CCPD. I need you to radio your dispatch and give them this location. Tell them to call 911 and report this to the police. Tell them officer needs assistance. Thank you."

Moments later, Kat removed the whiskey bottle from the back pocket of the man's pants. She had felt it as she purposely stumbled from the bus. Her timing was right on. Not only did she get a chance to feel around for evidence as she landed on the man, but her body on top of his prevented him from resisting as she closed the handcuffs around his wrists.

Kat turned the guy over with a quick jerk and reached into his jacket pocket to remove his wallet. "Well, well, well. What have we have here? It looks like you have two IDs, mister. Which one's yours?"

"I don't have two IDs, lady. My name's Benito Villarreal. Why are you on top of me, and why am I in handcuffs? I haven't done anything wrong."

"That'll be a matter for the jury to decide … Mr. Villarreal, is it?" Kat read him his rights and waited for help to arrive. Moments later, she hears sirens approaching from two different directions. She asked the bus driver for her name and then told her to continue on her route.

"Someone from PD will contact you later for a statement," Kat said.

The driver closed the door, and the bus disappeared into the darkness. Seconds later, help arrived. Kat identified herself and told the responding officers that she had just bagged the Skid Row Killer.

15

Kat rode with another police officer as they followed the other cruiser carrying the Skid Row Killer back to the city jail to arrest and interrogate him. Once they arrived, the other officer said that the suspect had requested a lawyer on the way downtown. The interrogation would have to wait until then.

Kat decided to go home. She was tired; she hadn't had a full night's sleep in weeks. Her eyes closed the instant her body hit her bed, and they didn't open until the next morning, when Captain Moore called to congratulate her and to tell her to get her ass down to the police station for the press conference.

Press conference? Press conference. Press conference! She kept repeating the words over and over. This would be her first one—the first of many, she hoped. Kat hit the shower and danced across the floor as she dressed. Everything was working out as planned. She was making her mark in the world.

16

The police chief, Henry Gibson, was talking with Captain Moore and a few other officers when Kat arrived at the station. She recognized their names as being assistant chiefs. They all turned to her and offered congratulations when she entered the room.

"Wow!" Kat said … but not loud enough for anyone to hear. "This is really cool."

Moments later, reporters for all three TV stations in town and the newspaper, the *Caller Times*, started arriving and taking their places near the podium that had been set up. Instantly, Kat became a little nervous. She hadn't prepared a statement. What would she say?

It didn't matter; the chief stood at the podium while the other officers lined up behind him. Kat managed to find a spot at the end, near her captain.

Chief Gibson said, "Last night an individual suspected of being the Skid Row Killer was apprehended by the Corpus Christi Police Department. He is being detained in the city jail in an isolated cell. There was enough evidence found on him at the time of the arrest that the district attorney's office is planning to charge him with eleven counts of first-degree murder. His name is Benito Villarreal, a twenty-four-year-old college student."

The chief stepped away from the podium before a single reporter could ask a question.

"That's it?" Kat said to no one in particular. "That's the big press conference? He could have at least mentioned the name of the arresting officer. Shit, shit, shit, shit, shit, shit. Damn, I can't believe this fucking shit."

Captain Moore replaced the chief at the podium to field the questions from the press as the chief and assistant chiefs filed out of the room.

I guess they have important business to take care of, Kat thought snidely, *like whose paying for lunch at the Nueces Club today. Those bastards. I worked my ass off finding that perp, and all I get for it is a handshake?* Kat wondered if she looked as livid as she felt.

Kat left the press room and went straight to her car. *Alice, Texas, here I come. I quit. I fucking quit.* Halfway through the forty-five-minute trip to her parents' house, Kat finally simmered down enough to realize she wasn't going to quit. This was her calling.

She pushed a CD into the player, and Edwin McCain's "These Are the Moments" started playing. Kat advanced to the next song because this was a moment she wanted to forget.

By the time Kat hit Alice city limits, she was singing along with Pat Benatar's "Hit Me with Your Best Shot," her favorite song on her CD mix. She preferred the older songs, even as a teenager. All her girlfriends thought she was weird that way. Kat stopped the music as she pulled into the driveway at her parents' house. She couldn't stay but a minute; she had to get back to work.

As Kat walked through the front door, she looked through the window in the dining room and saw her dad mowing the backyard. Her mother was standing over the sink in the kitchen, washing dishes. Kat sneaked up behind her and startled her as she wrapped her arms around her mom and lifted her off the floor. She loved her mom, but she was much closer to her dad. They seemed to be of the same spirit.

Her mom gave Kat a glass of lemonade to take outside to her dad. Kat knew that he would prefer a beer, but she took the lemonade anyway. Her dad turned off the mower as soon as Kat stepped out the back door.

"What's the matter, mija?"

He knows—he always knows—when something is bothering me.

She didn't answer. Instead, she said, "Just passing through town on police business. Thought I'd stop to say hi."

Ten minutes later, Kat was in her Mustang, heading due east, back to Corpus.

18

As Kat passed through Agua Dulce and Robstown, she was aware of where she was but was oblivious to everything else. She seemed to be driving on autopilot as she planned her future with the Corpus Christi Police Department. And what a future Kat envisioned for herself. It seemed only appropriate that "The Future's So Bright I Gotta Wear Shades," the last song on her CD, came on as she pulled into the parking lot at the police station.

She went up the elevator and back to her desk as though nothing had happened. But something had happened—to Kat, anyway. It would just take a while for all the pieces to fall together. No matter. She took great pleasure in knowing what was *about* to happen next.

A couple of her fellow detectives offered to buy her drinks after work in celebration of her making the arrest. As hard as it was to turn down free drinks, she declined, saying her mom wasn't feeling well and that she needed to check on her. She didn't need another coworker getting drunk and embarrassing himself by trying to get into her pants.

Besides, she was intoxicated already—high on her plan for a better life, and that life started today.

Over the next two years, Kat focused so much on her job that she neglected her personal life. She didn't have time for men. At least, that's what she told herself every day as she drove to work. Success first; then she could find the right guy, not Dr. Dickhead, teaching at some community college. She even stopped driving to Alice to visit her parents on Sunday. "If I'm going to be the best, I need to be working my cases, even on my days off," she would tell her dad whenever he called.

Kat's commitment was paying off. She solved every case she was given. She was like a forensic guru. One case involved a sixteen-year-old girl who had been strangled and left tied to a chain-link fence at one of the city parks. Kat recognized that a fresh load of dirt had just been dumped and that the consistency of the soil was different from the clay soil indigenous to Corpus Christi. She took samples, and when a lead pointed her to one of the girl's uncles, she scraped the wheel well above the tires on his car and found soil that matched that left at the park. A search warrant was issued, and they found more of the same type of soil in the treads of his tennis shoes. That alone wouldn't have been enough to convict the uncle, but Kat came through once again by finding a hair bow stuffed under his bed. Strands of hair were still in the bow, some of which had roots attached. With those, they could run a DNA analysis to see if it matched the victim.

"He ripped it right off her head," the identification tech told Kat.

"I'd like to rip something off that bastard," Kat mumbled.

The DNA found in the bow matched that of the young girl. The evidence was presented to the uncle, and he confessed when the district attorney offered a life sentence rather than going for the death penalty.

Kat was a little disgruntled that she wouldn't get to testify in court to put that son of a bitch away, but it had its upside. She would have been tied up with going over her testimony. His confession freed her up to work other cases.

20

Kat's next case proved to be a little more involved. A team of students from the university were doing research in the dunes on Padre Island, looking for new nesting grounds being used by the Kemp's ridley sea turtles, when they happened upon a dead body. The victim was female, probably late twenties or early thirties. Age was difficult to determine at the scene because of the accelerated decomposition due to the heat.

The victim appeared to have been cut twice, once in the neck and also in the chest. No weapons were found at the scene. Kat waded right in while some of the other officers stood at a distance, upwind of the rotting cadaver. Kat took photographs of the body and close-up shots of the wounds, but she waited on the medical examiner's investigator to arrive before she processed the body any further.

Ric Diaz, the chief investigator, arrived within thirty minutes, and Kat was relieved to see him. He was good. She had taken some of his classes at Del Mar College.

"What's shaking, Kitty-Kat?" He always teased her.

"Looks like she was killed someplace else and bled out some before they dragged the body here. I've got other officers searching the dunes in hopes of finding where she was killed."

"Hope they don't run into any rattlesnakes," Ric replied. "The dunes are full of them. You ready to do this?"

Ric was methodical. Kat had remembered him saying in his class, "You have to establish a system, and stick with it. You do it the same way, over and over, until it becomes so ingrained that you don't feel right doing it any other way. That way you cover all the bases without forgetting to do something simple, like taking the ambient temperature."

Kat had taken this advice to heart and was able to process a crime scene without having to refer to a checklist to see if she had left anything out. The routine also allowed her the freedom to think outside the box as she went through her steps.

"The wounds appear to have occurred postmortem," Ric said. "Scavengers, maybe coyotes or javelinas. From the looks of things, I'd say she's been here four, maybe five days." Ric pointed to the mounds of maggots gorging themselves on the helpless flesh.

As Kat kneeled down, she noticed something peculiar. "Take a look at the different stages of instars. Compare those in the mouth and chest with the ones on the neck."

"Good eye, Kitten. Let's collect some samples and see what comes flying at us." Ric laughed at his own joke. "Those in the mouth and chest appear to be in the third instar, while those around the neck are first instar."

Kat knew that an instar was a way of determining the different stages of a maggot's life cycle. Flies had been documented as arriving within fifteen minutes after death to lay their eggs in every opening in the body, natural or otherwise. They especially liked stab wounds, where the larvae had easy access to unprotected flesh.

Ric had told Kat that some of the Confederate doctors during the Civil War noticed that wounded soldiers previously left for dead had wounds that healed faster and with little or no infection if maggots were found eating the affected area around their wounds. The doctors even started using the maggots on infected wounds because the maggots could get deeper into the wound than any topical ointment known to medicine at the time. The use of maggots to fight off infections, however, was soon discontinued after the war. It seemed that just the thought of using maggots was so distasteful that most people would rather risk losing an arm or leg than have maggots eat away on them.

Kat assisted Ric as he collected maggots from the different affected areas. Ric took a temperature reading of the maggot mass teaming inside the mouth of the victim. "A swarm of maggots generate a lot more heat than you might think," Ric announced. "This temperature and the samples we collected will help narrow down the postmortem interval."

None of the other officers would get anywhere near the body, and since they couldn't use a gurney in the sand, Kat helped Ric load the victim into a black body bag and drag it to the beach, where Benny Moreno was waiting to transport the body to the medical examiner's office. Benny was nearing sixty years of age and had been transporting bodies for Nueces County since he was sixteen. He had started helping his dad transport bodies to funeral homes on weekends and during the summer, but when his dad suddenly had a heart attack and passed away, Benny quit school and assumed the role his dad had played for as long as he could remember. There was really no competition in those days, and when the Nueces County medical examiner's position was established in 1970, Benny seemed the logical choice to transport the bodies.

21

Once back in his office, Ric called upon Roxanne Abben, one of fifteen forensic entomologists in the entire United States. She just happened to call Corpus Christi home. She had chosen to move to Corpus because she thought her services would be best utilized there. As it turned out, there were not enough murders in a town of three hundred thousand that needed a forensic entomologist, so she paid her bills by teaching classes and using her biology degree to supervise the environmental aspects of offshore drilling rigs in the Gulf of Mexico.

"Yes, yes, I put the live ones into separate containers," Ric told Roxanne over the phone. Once he had placed all the insects into the same collection bottle, only to find out when he got back to the lab that one of the specimens was very aggressive and had eaten all the other specimens, both dead and alive. Roxanne never let him forget that mistake.

Ric said goodbye and told Kat that Roxanne would be there in twenty minutes to take the samples back to her lab to determine the species of flies that had laid the eggs and to help determine how long the body had been exposed to the elements.

Kat made a few phone calls to find out if any of the other officers had found the actual murder scene. No luck. She requested that an ID tech come over to collect fingerprints to see if they could identify the victim. She told the tech, "Bring some saline solution to get the prints. She is decomposed, and the fingers are starting to shrivel up."

The tech would have to inject the shriveled fingers of the victim with a special solution to help fill them out so a recognizable fingerprint could be taken.

She remembered a time when a body was found in such a state of decomposition that the skin slipped right off the hands as Kat tried to fingerprint her. Kat had slid her gloved hand into the glove of skin that came off the victim and had inked and rolled the victim's fingers as though they were her own. She had read about that in text books, and Ric had mentioned it in class, but Kat never actually thought she would do it in real life. *Oh, the price you pay to be the best.*

22

Roxanne was waiting for them when Kat and Ric finally arrived at the ME's office. She signed off on the chain of custody and placed the maggot specimens collected at the scene into a small ice chest to transport them back to her house on the river, where the entire second floor was set up as a laboratory. Roxanne was a striking women—five foot six, flowing blonde hair, and big, beautiful green eyes. Kat had been jealous of Roxanne's shapely body the first time they met, but Roxanne's laid-back approach to life quickly charmed Kat, and the two soon became friends.

"You wanna come over and help me get these babies prepped?" Roxanne asked.

"You betcha," Kat answered.

Roxanne might have been easygoing about most things, but she was serious about her work—deadly serious. Kat knew she could learn a lot from Roxanne, and it seemed that Roxanne never minded showing off her knowledge as it pertained to solving homicides.

Ric gladly handed off the brown paper sack he had used to transport the bottles containing the maggots. "You two run along now," he said. "I've got some real work that needs to be done—like identifying the body. Y'all have fun."

23

When they arrived at Roxanne's lab, she instructed Kat to immediately begin heating up water. "While you are doing that, I'm going to prepare the aquariums to let the live ones continue with their feast. I need to confirm my determination of which species these maggots belong to," Roxanne said.

Kat knew the hot water would be used to preserve some of the living maggot samples so they could be studied and identified under magnification. She had taken a class that Roxanne had taught at Del Mar College as an adjunct professor.

Once the prepping was completed it was time to look at the actual samples.

"Damn, this is odd!" Roxanne exclaimed.

"What is?"

"There are two completely different species here."

"What's so unusual about that?" Kat asked.

"Well, these two species happen to live in two completely different environments. This one here is Tabanidae diptera, a horsefly, which lives where the body was found, so no surprise there. But the one on the right is a bluebottle fly. Their preferred habitat is not out in the sunshine but protected from the sun, like in the woods.

"You think she could have been killed in the woods and then moved to the dunes?" Kat asked. "There was a lack of blood at the dunes where the body was found."

"Could have been. As a matter of fact, I think that has a high probability of being exactly what happened to our victim. I need to do a little more checking, but that would explain why those two species are in such completely different instars." Roxanne thought for a moment and then said, "It's possible that she was killed in a wooded area and left there for *over* forty-eight hours and then transported to the dunes for some unknown reason. The maggots from the black fly are in much younger stages."

Kat said, "I'm going to call Ric and see where he stands on identifying our girl."

24

With no personal identification found on the victim and her prints not found in any database, Ric turned to the missing persons file.

When Kat called, he told her, "Well, I found a possible match for sex and approximate age for a Marie Chavez, who was reported missing three days ago. I asked the father to come in to try to make a positive identification. He's on his way; he wanted to pick up his wife first. Will let you know whenever I know, kitten."

Thirty minutes later, Ric called back. "We got an ID."

Kat could hear crying in the background. "I'll be right there," Kat said. "Don't let the parents leave. I need to ask them some questions and quick." Kat then told Roxanne, "I'll be back in a bit. I need to interview the victim's parents before they leave the ME's office."

"Not a problem. I've got plenty to do here. See you in a bit. Pick up a six-pack on the way back; how about it?"

"I'll get two." Kat winked as she left.

Once at the ME's office, Kat introduced herself and asked the victim's parents, Mr. and Mrs. Chavez, to walk with her to the conference room so they could have some privacy.

"First, let me say I am very sorry for your loss, and we are going to do everything possible to catch whoever did this to your daughter."

"We know who did this," said Mr. Chavez. "It was that no-good cracker of a boyfriend."

"What's his name?" Kat asked.

"Darrell Willis. He drives a truck for Eagle Ford Shale. She was going to break it off. I can't believe my baby girl is gone," Mr. Chavez said.

"Where does this Darrell Willis live?" Kat asked.

"Down on Ocean Drive. Sundown Apartments. I don't know the number," Mrs. Chavez said.

Kat nodded. "We can find that. I will be paying this Darrell a visit shortly. You say Marie was about to end the relationship? Why?"

Mrs. Chavez took a tissue from her pocket and wiped her eyes. "Once he got this new job, he was gone all week long, and all he wanted to do on weekends was get drunk and smoke dope. Marie didn't use drugs, and after she realized she could not get him to stop, she wanted out."

"When was the last time you talked with your daughter?"

"Friday. She called during her lunch break to say she was meeting Darrell later that day to end it," Mrs. Chavez said. "I told her not to meet him, just end it over the phone, but she said that was chicken shit and that she would meet him at Water Street Oyster Bar so there would be plenty of people around if it went badly."

"That was the last time you two talked?" Kat.

"She called me later that evening," Mr. Chavez said, "to say she'd had a change of heart. Darrell promised to give up the drugs, so they were going camping for the weekend at Choke Canyon. She said she would call on Sunday on the way back since there would be no cell phone service in that area. She never called, and her phone went straight to voice mail when we tried to call her. We went to her apartment; she wasn't there. That's when we called the police."

"What did Marie do for a living?"

"She was a legal assistant for Octavio Ramirez."

Kat recognized the name. Octavio Ramirez was a prominent lawyer not only in Corpus but all of South Texas. "How well did she get along with her coworkers?" Kat asked.

"Everyone loved Marie," said Mrs. Chavez. "She was very outgoing and always made friends easily."

"Did she mention any legal cases that might not have turned out so well?"

"No, Marie never talked about her work, so we didn't pry," Mr. Chavez answered. "I'm telling you it was that damn Darrell! That's who killed Marie, and if you don't do something about it, I will."

"I'm headed there right now. You stay out of this," Kat warned. "No need to complicate things. Let me take care of it." With that, Kat excused herself and headed out the door. She called Roxanne to tell her she would be a little later getting back than expected but that she would stop off at Cotton's and pick up some ribs for dinner. Everybody loved Cotton's BBQ.

Kat showed her badge to the manager of the Sundown Apartments, a middle-aged Hispanic woman who was about as big around as she was tall. She didn't even rise from her chair to greet Kat. She just typed in Darrell Willis's name and said, "Twelve B, the second building on the right. Upstairs. He's never home during the week, though."

The Buddha of a manager was correct—no answer at 12B. Kat would have to contact Eagle Ford Shale to find the whereabouts of Darrell Willis. She checked the time on her phone. *Seven o'clock. No one will be in the office. Okay, first thing tomorrow.*

Roxanne acted as though she was starving when Kat finally arrived with the beer and ribs. "Damn, girl, didn't think you would ever get here. Let's eat."

Before they finished their first beer, Roxanne shared her preliminary discovery. "Okay, it looks like our vic was killed late Friday night, possibly early Saturday morning—let's call it midnight. She lay in a wooded area for two days, and then, for some reason, she gets moved to the dunes, where she remained until she was found by the university students on Wednesday morning. The stages of the bluebottle fly maggots are so much more advanced than the Tabanidae flies that they were laid at least two days before the horseflies got to her."

"Well, that timeline goes well with what the vic's parents said. She was last known to be with her soon-to-be ex-boyfriend, Darrell Willis, on Friday night. No one has heard from her since."

"So did you talk with our Mr. Willis?" asked Roxanne.

"Wasn't home. He works for Eagle Ford Shale. I'll hit him up tomorrow. Nothing else we can do tonight." Kat grinned. "Feel like getting wasted?"

"You read my mind, baby girl."

25

Over their third beer, Kat asked Roxanne, "What's one of your most interesting cases?" Kat loved drinking with Roxanne. Once the alcohol took effect, Roxanne would share stories.

"Well, this one is not far off. Pretty unusual circumstances here, but I do recall one case in Hawaii, where I did my graduate work with Dr. Wells. I assisted him with a case in which a twenty-five-year-old woman was reported missing. Her car was found in a remote pineapple field two days later. There was blood spatter in the car that indicated the driver was shot by someone sitting in the back seat. The blood belonged to the missing woman. Her body was discovered six months later, partially buried near where her car was found. Dr. Wells was called in because there was an abundant amount of entomological evidence."

Kat laughed. "Is that the politically correct way to say *maggots*?"

"Maggots, flies, cheese skippers—you name it, it was there," Roxanne said.

"Cheese skippers?"

"Oh yes, thin, long larvae that can jump two feet into the air. They get on your clothes. I hate it when they jump into my face."

"How do they jump?"

"It's a defense mechanism to escape predators that like to come late to the party, once the maggots get things rocking, like carrion beetles. They bend the anterior portion of their bodies all the way backward to their posterior end. When they release, they spring into the air. Not very pleasant to work with, but I'm told that some cheeses in Europe are not considered fit to eat until the cheese skippers arrive; hence, the name."

"Sounds awful. What happened with the case?"

"The police had a suspect, and they wanted us to confirm how long the body had been there. Our calculations indicated that she couldn't have been there more than nine days. That seemed to really piss off the detective working the case. He proceeded to tell Dr. Wells that he didn't know what he was talking about. That the body had been buried since December and that some animals probably had uncovered a portion of it, and then the insects arrived. He said they were certain the victim was shot in December. With the exception of the entomological record, all the other evidence pointed to the detective's conclusion. To make matters worse, the suspect had been incarcerated that spring and had been in prison for another crime ever since. We, in effect, gave him an alibi. I distinctly remember going with Dr. Wells to the DA's office to discuss our findings. While there, I saw some of the photographs taken from the burial site before we arrived. There was a large amount of some white substance near the body that was not there by the time we arrived. I asked what it was, and the detective scoffed, 'That's lime. The farmer probably used it in his field to help grow his crops.'

"Dr. Wells took exception to the detective's being so dismissive. He said, 'Did you ask the farmer if he used lime? That's not common in a pineapple field.' Turned out no one had checked with the farmer, so Dr. Wells asked if we could test the white substance. They agreed, so we took a sample over to the university chemistry lab immediately. The white substance turned out to be a fungus. It was growing all around the partially buried body. After death, it's the odors that attract the flies to the body. These odors dissipate after three weeks, whether the body is buried or not. That's why Dr. Wells established a timeline of nine days, rather than six months. The odors from the body would not have been present to attract the flies if it had been there since December.

"But—and this is a big *but*—the fungus that was present gives off an odor that is very similar to that of a rotting corpse, which is why the flies were attracted to the fungus. They found the corpse and laid their eggs, just as nature had guided them to do. Once we established the flies were attracted to the fungus rather than the body, Dr. Wells amended his findings to indicate that the body had been buried for several months, as was evidenced by the amount of fungus that was present around the body. The suspect was brought to trial, and based on the other evidence collected by the police, he was found guilty and now is serving a life sentence."

"Wow, so you actually had a hand in solving the case," Kat said.

"Oh well, what can I say? I am the best forensic entomologist in Corpus Christi." Roxanne laughed.

"You are the *only* one in Corpus—hell, even the state. How many forensic entomologists are there, anyway?"

"Last time I checked there were sixteen in the United States, but one of those has passed away. Can't say for certain, but I know there are not very many of us. You'd think we would get paid more. Maybe we should form a union. The pay for this job is for shit."

26

The next morning Kat called the main office of Eagle Ford Shale and spoke with one of the managers, Mr. Calvin Winston. He told Kat that Darrell Willis was indeed one of their employees and that he was en route somewhere between Kennedy and Floresville at the moment. They expected him back in George West, where their trucks were dropped off each day, around six that evening.

Guess I'm having dinner in George West tonight, Kat thought. The hour's drive north would give her a chance to collect her thoughts. This wasn't the only case Kat was working at the moment, but it was the one that stayed in the back of her mind as she turned on her computer to start her day.

She had spent the night at Roxanne's.

"Hey, you awake?" Kat said softly as she was getting ready to leave.

"You just busted in on me and Brad Pitt skinny-dipping. Damn," said Roxanne.

"Sounds like a sweet dream. Now get your ass up, and give me something more that I can use to nail whoever killed our vic."

"I thought you said the boyfriend did it."

Kat shook her head. "The *father* said the boyfriend did it. You know I can't jump to conclusions like that. I gather as much evidence as possible, and my interpretation of such evidence leads me to a conclusion. Now tell Brad sweet dreams; you'll see him tonight. Get me some more evidence—*pleeease*."

Kat had booted up her computer and now saw one of her three open investigations front and center. A forty-two-year-old female named Margarete Leos had been reported missing two weeks ago. Not much to go on. The husband didn't report her as being missing. The report came from her adult children when they could not reach her by phone, and she was not in her home.

When questioned, the husband said that she had disappeared twice before, one time for nearly a month. He didn't seem too concerned. "I figure she'll come back when the money runs out," he said.

Her children had confirmed what the husband said, but something didn't sit right with Kat.

She's not used her credit card, Kat thought, *which she* did *use on the two previous times she ran away. What makes a person just up and take off?*

She called the husband. "Mr. Leos, this is Officer Gonzales with CCPD. You may remember me. I'm working the case of your wife's disappearance. How are you today?"

"Oh sí, sí, I remember you," he said in a heavy Hispanic accent. "Anything?"

"I would like to come out again and take a look around, if you don't mind. I'm wondering if there's something we might have missed that would help us find her."

"I'm working, but I call my daughter. She can come over to let you in."

Kat thought he sounded a little more concerned than he had the previous times they had talked. She drove over to the west side of Corpus Christi to see if something hit her that hadn't jumped out at her on the other times. Mrs. Leos's twenty-year-old daughter, Angie Quesada, met Kat at her parents' house. Two small children—Kat guessed them to be two and three years old—stood on either side of their mother. *Presumably guarding her hips*, Kat thought.

"Got any news on my mom?" Angie asked.

"She has not been using her credit card this time around, and that strikes me as odd. Seems she maxed it out last time before returning home, so I'm here to take another look around. Thanks for meeting me here. I know it's not easy, getting everyone ready on such short notice."

"No problem. I'm just glad that someone is doing something about it this time," Angie replied. "Last time, no one even came out. They just took down the information over the phone."

Kat had already spoken to all the family members on her previous trips, so she just smiled and headed into the house. There was a noticeable difference in housekeeping between this time and the last time Kat had been there. *Well, he wasn't expecting company*, Kat thought.

The daughter apologized for the mess. Other than the mess, the house appeared to be about the same as before. Kat went through the kitchen and out into the backyard. There was a hint of smoke in the air that was stronger there in the back. "Where's that smoke coming from?" she asked.

Angie pointed across the yard. "Poppa. He's started burning his trash. We told him it's bad for the environment, but he does it anyway."

"That barrel wasn't here the last time. When did he start doing that?" Kat asked.

"A few days after Mom left. She would never let him do something like that."

Kat ventured over to the barrel, waving the smoke out of her face as she did so. "You know it's against the law to burn trash within the city limits. Please inform your dad that this cannot continue."

"We know. My brother and I thought that someone would report him. He had some really big fires going all through the night when he first started. He says it calms him. I didn't know that he had that much trash to burn."

Kat found a hose lying next to the house and turned on the spigot. "I'm going to put this out. It's not safe to leave it this way."

Once the fire was extinguished, Kat kicked the barrel over on its side. It rolled away from the muddy spot in the backyard. Using a towel from the clothesline, she turned the barrel completely upside down to dump out the smoldering trash. After rummaging through the debris, Kat found what had been eluding her in this case—physical evidence.

Several human teeth and what appeared to be parts of bone were partially covered by the burned trash.

"What … are those?" Angie asked, stepping closer. "Oh my God, no! He didn't. Oh my God!" She quickly ushered her children around to the front of the house.

Kat called ID to come process the remains in the barrel and asked for another officer to arrest Mr. Leos while she waited for the crime scene techs to arrive.

"Damn." That was about all she could say.

27

Later that day, on her way to talk with Darrel Willis, Kat got a call from Roxanne.

"I may have something for you, love."

Kat laughed. "Don't give me that *love* crap. What you got?"

"I found a species of tick making itself at home among the pubs."

"What the hell is that?"

"A very special tick. It lives on the deer and javelina that roam around Choke Canyon. I mean, they are found elsewhere, but that's the only place in Texas."

"Smoking gun?" Kat asked.

"Damn straight, darling."

With that, Kat knew she would not be trying the cuisine in George West, at least not that night. She also knew that she would not be making the trip back to Corpus alone.

Kat waited with Calvin Winston until almost six thirty. That's when Darrel Willis drove his truck onto the lot. Kat wasted no time; as soon as Darrel stepped down from his eighteen-wheeler, Kat walked up to him with her hand on her pistol.

"Darrel Willis?" she said in her firmest voice.

"Yes. What's this about?"

"I'm placing you under arrest, sir. Please turn around and place your hands on the truck," Kat said as she frisked and cuffed Darrel.

"Arrest? Arrest for what?"

"For the murder of Marie Chavez. Now get in the back seat."

Kat was prepared if Darrel had tried to use his six-foot five frame to resist her, but he seemed so shocked and nervous that he just sat down in the back seat of her cruiser.

Kat radioed ahead to apprise dispatch of her situation and estimated time of arrival. She didn't need help but wouldn't mind having other officers meet her to escort Darrel inside police headquarters.

Kat felt like her planets were lining up. Damn, where was that CD with Timbuk 3 singing "The Future's So Bright I Gotta Wear Shades"? She would gladly have cranked it up.

28

Mr. Leos confessed to killing his wife and burning the remains in his new trash barrel. It seemed that Mrs. Leos had returned home about a week after her last disappearance. Enraged that her home was in such disarray, she flew into Mr. Leos, hitting and biting him. Mr. Leos insisted he fought back in self-defense, that he struck her in the head with a shovel as she followed him into the backyard. She collapsed immediately and did not move. He knew that she was probably dead, but he didn't want to call the police and risk going to jail, so he did the first thing that came to mind—he cut her up and burned her in the barrel. This was the secondhand story Kat got from Detective Timms, who was handling the Mr. Leos's interrogation while Kat was in with Darrel Willis.

Darrell Willis put on a front in the beginning. "Why am I here? I've not done nothin'."

Kat again read Darrel his Miranda rights so it would be on video for the record. Then she said, "Look, we have witnesses willing to testify that you were with Marie last Friday night at Water Street Oyster Bar and that you two left that same day to go camping at Choke Canyon. We have verification from the agents there, who have said you and one other party rented one of the cabins for the weekend. We know you took her there. You killed her and hid her in the woods later that night. We have evidence to prove that. Then, for some reason, you took her body to the dunes and dumped her Sunday night. She was found three days later. How am I doing so far?"

Darrel's eyes widened, and he shifted in his seat. "How … how do you know these things? Did one of the other campers use their phone to video?"

At that moment, Kat knew the confession was next. "Why did you move her to the dunes? Why not just leave her at Choke Canyon?"

Darrel sighed heavily. "Too many javelinas everywhere. I was afraid they would drag her body out into the open. I didn't mean to kill her; it was an accident. I was drunk and went out by the fire to smoke some weed. When she came out of the cabin, she smelled it and I knew it was over between us. She started yelling like she was going to report me to the park rangers there. I hit her in the mouth with my fist to shut her up. Her head must have hit one of the rocks around the fire pit 'cause she didn't move. I felt for a pulse. Nothing. I had to do something, so I carried her as far back into the woods as I could and covered her with limbs and leaves. I drove home that night. I started getting worried, so I went back Sunday night and got her. It was hard finding her in the dark. Something had been rooting around her, so I took her to the most desolate place I could access—the dunes. I'm sorry. I didn't mean for this to happen."

"Well, Mr. Willis, I can think of another desolate place, and I believe you will be spending the rest of your life there. And guess what? It's just down the road from Choke Canyon."

29

"Wow, you kicked ass, girlfriend," Roxanne said when she got the call from Kat. "Sounds like a T-Head kind of night. I'm buying."

"Roger that," Kat said. "Have to tell you I'm riding high at the moment. Won't take much."

Roxanne laughed. "Good, 'cause I'm only buying the first round. It's up to you to shake that ass and get us enough free beers from all the hard-dicks. Pick you up at ten?"

"Make it eleven. I'm still finishing up here, and then I gotta shower and change."

"We're taking tomorrow off, are we?"

"Damn straight I'm taking tomorrow off after a day like this," Kat said.

But deep down inside, she knew she would be at work tomorrow. It's what she lived for.

30

Three hours of sleep was not enough. Kat hit the snooze button when the alarm sounded at six o'clock. Finally, she managed to crawl into the shower at seven and made it to work by eight. *Bright-eyed and bushy-tailed*, she kept telling herself. *At least it's Friday, and I can catch up on sleep tonight.* She didn't want to miss seeing Captain Moore smile when he learned she solved two cases in the same day.

Captain Moore placed a cup from Starbucks on her desk as he passed by on the way to his office. He didn't say a word.

"Damn, do I look that bad?" Kat muttered.

Her colleague, Detective Javier Aguilar, chuckled. "I'm not touching that one, hun. That's between you and the captain. By the way, nice job yesterday."

"Coffee? He brings me coffee? For real? That's it? Damn! I thought at the very least I'd get a smile. But no-o-o-o. It's coffee. What's a girl gotta do to get some recognition around here anyway?"

The other detectives immediately became engrossed in their computer screens.

Kat picked up her coffee, let out a "Well, fuck this," and walked out of the office. She held back tears as she sat in her car in the parking lot, trying to decide if she would drive to Alice or just call Roxanne and unload.

Roxanne picked up first ring.

"I can't believe this shit!" Kat raged.

"What?" Roxanne asked.

"Captain Moore." She took a deep breath and exhaled loudly. "He put Starbucks on my desk."

"And that's a bad thing, I take it?"

"He didn't say one word to me. He just put the coffee on my desk and went into his office. He didn't say, 'Great job; you solved more cases yesterday than the whole unit did all week.' No, he didn't say one fucking word."

"Kitten, it's okay. Everyone knows what a terrific job you are doing. Don't let this one incident get blown out of proportion. You are awesome. I know it, you know it, and that dumb SOB Captain Moore knows it too, even if he didn't say anything today. He will; just give him a little time. Now get your ass back to work. You gotta make this place safe for me to go out at night."

Kat wiped her face. "You're right. Thanks. Sorry to go off like that. He just really pissed me off."

"BJ's tonight?" asked Roxanne.

"Sorry, not tonight. I still have to catch criminals, remember."

31

"Hey, bitch, guess who I just got off the phone with?" Roxanne said.

"Brad Pitt," Kat said.

"No, that was yesterday. I'm talking about today."

"Just tell me already," Kat said, with much less enthusiasm than Roxanne wanted. Kat heard a click as Roxanne hung up on her. She sat there, stunned, for almost a minute before she called Roxanne back. "Sorry. I'm still a little pissed off with Captain Moore."

"You still hanging on to that shit? Fuck him," Roxanne said. "You gotta learn to let go, girl. They don't pay you enough to get ulcers."

"I know. It's just that I was expecting a lot more. Oh well, tell me. Who the hell have you been talking to?"

"*Texas Monthly*."

"What? *Texas Monthly*. Why would you be talking to them?"

"I used to be friends with one of the writers, Adan Cisneros."

Kat laughed. "You mean you used to fuck one of the writers."

"Shut up. So what? Anyway, as I was about to say before I was so rudely interrupted, I called him and told him that you solved the Marie Chavez case, using my expertise of course."

"Of course," Kat chimed in.

"Are you going to keep interrupting, or do you just not want to hear this?"

"Sorry, last time. I promise."

"Let me tell you what he said. He wants to come to Corpus and do a feature story on you and me. Can you believe it? *Texas* fuckin' *Monthly* wants to put our pictures in every newsstand in Texas. We will be famous."

"So now maybe we could get laid. Is that it?" Kat said.

"Speak for yourself, sister. I don't have any problem in that department. Any night of the week, I can get whatever I want. And you could too … if you just would."

Kat sniffed. "I would rather dodge the herpes-and-HPV scene, thank you very much."

"You know I've heard of this little invention called a condom. You might Google it, and check it out sometime. You are so uptight over this Captain Moore thing. You need to go out and get laid."

"Spoken like a true male," said Kat. "Are you sure you don't have a Y chromosome? Oh, by the way, that invention you mentioned doesn't stop HPV. You don't need intercourse to get it, and 90 percent of sexually active people either have it or have had it. No such thing as truly safe sex these days."

"Are you kidding me? Ninety percent? Whoa, Nellie. That can't be right, can it?"

"Google it, bitch," Kat said with a laugh. "Now tell me more about your man at *Texas Monthly*."

"Okay, back on track. He wants to interview us, and he wants to do a ride-along with you. You know, see the Queen of Homicide in action. What do you say about that?"

Kat couldn't believe her ears. "Holy shit." The long hours and sacrifice of a personal life were finally paying off. "I can't wait to tell Captain I-Don't-Give-a-Shit Moore about this. When does he want to come?"

"Next week. I'm going to get my hair done and hit the tanning bed. You in?"

"Hell yeah!"

32

"Hell no!" Captain Moore said when Kat approached him with the news. That was not the response she had anticipated. Boiling over, she asked, "Why the fuck not?"

"Talking like that to your superiors can get you fired," Captain Moore fired back. "You need to get a grip, and I mean fast."

"You're right. I was out of line, and I'm sorry. Now can you please tell me why we can't do the interview with *Texas Monthly*?"

"The Bug Lady can talk to whomever she wants. She is used as a consultant only. Need I remind you she is not actually part of the police force?"

"Okay, then what's the problem with me doing an interview?"

"You *are* part of the police force, and since you *are* part of this department, you will not call attention to yourself. Do I make myself clear on this matter?"

Kat shook her head. "Not exactly. I don't understand it. I thought it would be good publicity for *our* department."

"Look, singling you out of all the other deserving detectives will just create bad blood. It will cause turmoil in this office, and we don't need that, just so you can parade around with some writer from *Texas Monthly*. There are a lot of good cops here. They do their jobs; they solve cases too. Do they expect to get *their* pictures on the cover of a magazine every time they close a case? No, they just go to work on the next one, and that's exactly what you ought to do right now. This conversation is over."

With that, Captain Moore did an about-face, walked into his office, and shut the door behind him.

Stunned, Kat sat down at her desk and stared at her computer monitor. The screen was full of words, none of which were comprehensible. She was off into her own little world.

Roxanne's friend did the interview with her, and she and Kat both awaited the next issue of *Texas Monthly* with great anticipation.

Kat reluctantly declined the many requests to interview her, not giving a reason. Things were extremely tense between Captain Moore and her. They didn't speak to each other unless it was absolutely necessary, and they didn't make eye contact when they did. The other detectives picked up on it and kidded Kat about it. One morning there was a box of chocolates on Kat's desk when she arrived at work. The attached card read, "From Captain Moore," but as she looked at the bottom of the card, she saw the word *NOT*! The guys burst out laughing as she read it.

Kat was pissed but she wasn't going to show it. She took the box to the secretary in the outer office. "Here, Evelyn. The boys and I wanted to say thanks for doing such a great job." With that, Kat went straight back to her desk, booted up her computer, and refrained from saying a word to any of the jerks who unfortunately were her colleagues.

"Come on, Kat, you know that was funny. We didn't mean anything by it," Detective Huerta apologized.

Kat just looked up from her monitor, smiled, and went back to work. She left for lunch by herself. As soon as she hit the elevator, she called Roxanne. "I can't believe those assholes."

"What did they do this time?"

Kat explained and then invited Roxanne to lunch at Water Street Oyster Bar.

"Heck yes. I never turn down a free lunch, especially from there. Give me thirty to get there."

"Take your time," Kat said. "I'm gonna drive down Ocean. Maybe I'll pull over at Oleander Point and watch the kite surfers. I just need to decompress a minute or two. Call when you get close."

Kat drove down the most scenic street in the city. "Great. No wind. Fuck it. Maybe the dolphins will be out." Less than a mile from the police station, Kat pulled into Oleander Point and stared out over Corpus Christi Bay as she contemplated her next course of action. "I love living here—the sun, the beach. I'm not leaving. Those assholes need to get their acts together. Quit acting like junior high jerks. Note to self: Call Dad tonight. Better yet, go see him and Mom on Sunday."

34

At lunch with Roxanne, Kat decided not to talk about her issues with work. She would just move on and not let the trivial bother her any longer. *I'll still visit Dad and Mom on Sunday*, she thought. *Maybe even go to mass with them.*

"Where do you want to go tonight?" Roxanne asked.

"Somewhere fun. I need a night out on the town."

"That's my girl. Maybe we should pull a *Thelma and Louise*."

"Who are Thelma and Louise?" asked Kat.

"A movie. I forgot—you're too young. Doesn't matter; we are going to have a blast."

Kat didn't go out often, but when she did, she preferred going with Roxanne. It seemed everyone who was anyone knew Roxanne. They never waited in line to get into any club in town, and all the bartenders threw out her first drink for free. The men in the bar bought the rest.

Tonight is going to be one of those nights, Kat thought. Then she thought about how long it had been since she had gotten laid. *I've been married to the police force, and look where that's gotten me.* She started getting horny just thinking about her night out.

The sun rose in Kat's rearview mirror on Sunday morning as she drove to Alice to meet her parents for breakfast before mass. It had been months since her last visit. She made a promise to herself to not let that happen again. Her dad was not getting any younger, and she loved the way he counseled her. Her mom was wonderful, but she always had been a daddy's girl.

"Hi, Mom. How are you?" Kat said as she entered her childhood home without knocking. "Where's Dad?"

"In the shower, mija. How are you? Haven't seen you in a while."

"I know. I'm going to start calling more often during the week and get over here on the weekend on a more regular basis. Need any help?"

"Pour yourself a cup of coffee, and pull up a stool to the counter. I want to hear everything you've been up to. Got a boyfriend?"

Kat laughed. "No, Mom, no boyfriend. My job is my boyfriend."

"See how that keeps you company in your old age. Does your job keep your bed warm?"

"I get it. It's just not the right time in my life for that yet."

"Oh, when will it be the right time, Katarina?"

Kat didn't reply. This was one reason she was so much closer to her dad. He never prodded her about her love life. *As far as Dad is concerned,* Kat thought, *I'm still a virgin—a thirty-four-year-old virgin.*

Just then her dad came around the corner wearing slacks, socks, and a wife-beater undershirt, drying what little hair he had left with a towel. "Thought I heard voices. I was wondering if your mama had gone loco. So glad to see you, mija." He hugged and kissed her.

Kat almost started crying; she was going to miss this man when he was gone.

Breakfast was uneventful, and later, the priest seemed to drag on. Kat's mind began to wander. She reevaluated her life plan and decided to make a few tune-ups here and there. She would work out the details on the drive back to Corpus Christi.

And that she did.

36

Over the next week, Kat solved a few minor cases but nothing to write home about. The following Sunday morning, however, changed everything. Kat got an urgent call from the chief of police, requesting her presence immediately.

"There has been a death," he told her. "That's all I want to say over the phone. I'll fill you in as soon as you arrive. It's 236 Oleander Drive."

Kat quickly dressed—she knew that address. It was Captain Moore's residence.

She pulled up in front within fifteen minutes of receiving the call and was met by a uniformed officer as she crossed the front lawn. *What's so urgent?* she wondered. *There's no crime scene tape anywhere.*

"Good, you're finally here," Chief Henry Gibson greeted her, leading Kat toward the rear of the house. On the way, she saw her captain—Bob, as he liked to be called—sitting with the other detectives in the living room.

"What do we have here, Chief?" Kat asked.

Chief Gibson grimaced. "Marlana is dead. Bob found her in the pool this morning when he got up. They had been married twenty-five years."

"So why am I here? Is foul played suspected?"

"Hell no, of course not. But we have to conduct an investigation, just so the papers can't try to jam this up our asses later if we didn't follow proper protocol, just because a police officer's wife dies. Can't give preferential treatment, so I called you. Besides, all those other bastards in there were playing cards together last night. They can't be involved. The press would have a field day." He opened the door leading to the backyard.

Paramedics had already walked away from the body lying face up on the ground at the far end of the pool.

"So, Chief, this investigation is in my hands now, correct?" Kat asked. "I just want to clarify that."

"Yes, yes, this is in your hands now, Detective Gonzales."

"Well then, sir, I'm going to have to ask that you leave this scene and take those 'bastards,' as you so eloquently called them, with you. We already have had more than enough contamination here to jeopardize my investigation."

Chief Gibson turned to Kat, seemingly dumbfounded. "What?"

"I'm sorry, Chief, but you handed over this mess to me, and I'm trying to follow proper protocol. I hope you can appreciate my position. That being said, sir, I respectfully request that you and everyone else not involved in this investigation please vacate the premises." Kat smiled.

Without a word, Chief Gibson walked into the living room and told the other detectives, except Captain Moore, to leave, knowing full well Kat would have met with unnecessary resistance if she had asked.

Immediately, Kat called for ID to send a crime scene tech. She instructed the uniformed officer she'd met on the way in to set up two perimeters using crime scene tape. "One for the lookie-loos and the second farther out, to keep the press and general public away," she instructed.

"Yes, ma'am," he said.

"And one more thing—get a crime scene log started right away, before those detectives leave."

"Yes, ma'am."

"Yes, ma'am," she thought. *I never get tired of hearing that.* Kat walked over to inspect the body at the edge of the pool. She pulled out her phone and dialed a familiar number.

"Ric, got a DB. It's Captain Moore's wife. Found her this morning in the pool at her house. Can you stop by Starbucks on the way over? Chief Gibson called me personally this morning at the butt-crack of dawn. And a taco sure would be nice too, please. No chance for breakfast. Looks like I may be here awhile. Owe you big time."

"Still bean and avocado, darling?" Ric asked.

"My man, if you weren't already married, just think of the possibilities." Kat giggled.

"I don't even want to go there, kitten." Ric laughed.

Kat was so glad to have such a good working relationship with the medical examiner's office. Her cases always got top priority, and she had learned so much from Ric's classes and being beside him in the field.

Kat drank her coffee and ate her taco as she knelt down beside the body with Ric. "Can you determine approximate time of death?" Kat asked.

"Well, she'd been in the water awhile, see the livor mortis on her abdomen and thighs?" Ric pointed to the purplish discoloration on the front of Mrs. Moore's body. "It doesn't blanch," he said as he pushed his finger into the discolored area. "If it turned white with this pressure, pushing away the blood, and returned to purple once the pressure was released, I'd say less than six hours. It takes that long for the blood to congeal inside the body. But since the livor is fixed, I have to say at least six hours, maybe eight."

"What about the rigor mortis?' Kat asked. "I can see it forming in her jaw."

"Good eye, kitten," Ric said. "As you know, rigor begins to form in all the muscles at the same times as the actin and the myosin lock in place."

Kat nodded. "As I know well from your classes, rigor becomes apparent in the face, neck, and hands first because those muscles are small. The torso doesn't become rigid until hours later, since those muscles are so much larger."

Ric smiled. "That's why you were my top pupil. A long time ago they actually taught that the rigor began at the head and worked its way down through the body. We know better now. Comparing the rigor and the livor mortis, I'd say about eight hours, give or take one. So between ten and eleven last night. We can't use algor mortis since she's been in the water. She lost her heat fast. Even her core temperature is useless."

"You sure?" Kat asked.

"Well, it's not exact—there are too many variables—but yes, I'd say definitely before midnight but well after nine o'clock. Best I can do for you."

"Thanks, that's a start. Autopsy?" Kat asked.

"Not my call. I'll do a thorough external examination, once we get the body to the office, unless you come up with something indicating otherwise. I'll let you know what the ME decides. Keep me posted, and I'll do the same for you. How's the taco?"

"Thanks, totally awesome," Kat said in her best valley-girl voice. "I have to go inside and question Captain Moore, if we're done here."

"Yep. Benny is out front, waiting. I'll send him in so we can get her taken care of right away. Heard they were married for twenty-five years. Sad, real sad. Good guy, Captain Moore. You are fortunate to work for him."

"Yeah."

38

"Captain, I'm very sorry for your loss," Kat said softly. "You know the chief wants everything by the book on this, so even though it pains me to do so, I must ask you some questions. Okay?"

"I understand. Do your job," Captain Moore replied.

"Let's start with you discovering your wife's body and work backward from there."

"I got up this morning at my usual time—six o'clock. I went into the kitchen to make some coffee and grabbed the paper from the front while waiting on the coffee to finish. I usually go out by the pool to read before my wife wakes up."

"You didn't notice her missing in the bed this morning?" Kat asked.

"We sleep in separate bedrooms. Have been for the past two years."

Kat had heard the rumors but needed to confirm them. "Go on, Captain."

"I poured a cup, and as soon as I opened the back door, I saw Marlana facedown in the pool. I jumped in but immediately knew she was too far gone. I tried CPR; I just had to see if maybe a miracle could bring her back."

"How could you tell she was too far gone?" Kat asked.

"Cold. She was so cold. I knew she had been in the water too long, probably since last night."

"Okay, let's backtrack. What did you do last night?"

"I got home around eleven and went straight to my bedroom at that end of the house." Captain Moore pointed to the bedroom behind Kat. "I took a shower and read in bed for about thirty minutes or so. I turned the light off just around midnight."

"Where were you before that?"

"Playing poker with the boys. We usually play once or twice a month at somebody's house. We were at Javier's last night. I left around ten thirty, pretty much my usual time. I'm not much on poker, but we started playing when we were all fresh out of the academy, and it's my way of staying connected to them."

"When was the last time you saw Marlana alive?"

"We had dinner around six. She was excited about something. She said she would be a new woman soon, but she wouldn't let me know what was going on. We ate here, and I left at seven thirty to pick up beer and then headed over to Javier's."

"Nobody else was here when you left?" asked Kat.

"No, she was alone. She liked having some downtime to herself."

"Did Marlana go swimming by herself at night?"

"She used to. She would skinny-dip and surprise me when I got home. But that hasn't happened in at least five years, so no, she did not swim alone at night. I can't believe she did last night."

"You said she was excited about something, but did she show any signs that something had been troubling her?"

"No more than usual. She hadn't been herself for the last few years. I just attributed it to our getting older and her losing her sex drive."

Before Kat could ask questions about their sex life, she heard barking. "Is that your dog?"

"Marlana's. Name's Betsy. She's old; can't hear. She can barely get around. Let me go let her outside." Captain Moore got up and walked to the opposite end of the house to let the dog out of his wife's bedroom.

Kat followed, and as Captain Moore opened the door to the room, a silky terrier ran to the front door. She was carrying a syringe between her teeth. Kat quickly followed and gently removed the syringe from Betsy's mouth.

"Was Marlana diabetic?" Kat asked.

"No, but she asked me to pick up a syringe for her. I questioned her about it. She joked that she needed it for her heroin. I knew better, but she would not tell me why she really needed it. She just kept saying it would be a surprise and to stop asking because she didn't want to ruin it for me."

"So you purchased this syringe for her?" Kat asked.

"I asked one of the dieners at the ME's office to get me one. I didn't have time to stop off at CVS, and I damn sure didn't want to explain why I needed a syringe."

"So you asked a diener at the ME's office to float you a syringe. Only one? And which diener?"

"Marissa. And yes, Marlana said she only needed one, so that's all I got."

Kat smelled the empty syringe before placing it into an evidence bag. "Smells like it's been used. I'll have the lab analyze it to see if there is any residue left. You sure Marlana did not have a drug problem?"

"No, she did not, and I resent your suggesting otherwise."

"Captain, you know better than I that if Marlana did have issues that she would not have let you know about them."

"I know. How much longer are you going to be here?"

"Let me check with the techs and see. I'm going to run this over to the lab and get them working on this right away. I'll let you know what I find out."

With that, Kat walked outside to visit with the crime scene techs. Then she reentered the house. "They need another couple of hours, but I'm done here, unless you can think of anything else."

Captain Moore did not reply. He just cradled Betsy in his arms.

39

Kat climbed into her Mustang and headed straight to the crime lab at the Department of Public Safety, knowing full well the Corpus labs would have to send her syringe to DPS to have it tested. Her going to DPS herself also meant there would be no tampering with the evidence, as it would all be handled by the state rather than the city, ruling out any backlash later on if her investigation was reviewed—and she knew it would be.

She called ahead to see if William was working and was glad to hear him answer the phone at the lab. "I'm bringing over a syringe, and I need it tested to find out what was in it," she told him. "I'll be there in less than ten minutes. Can we do this right away?"

"Who is this?" William asked and then laughed. "Had you there for a moment, didn't I, Kat? Just fucking with you, baby girl. What's the rush?"

"Captain Moore's wife was found floating in their pool this morning. Looks like she was there overnight. Their dog was carrying this syringe in its mouth. I have an idea this may be more than just an accidental drowning, but I need some hard evidence to prove that. Can we do this stat and keep the results between you and me, just in case?"

"Bring it on. Text me when you get here so I can let you in. No one else is here on a Sunday, so it shouldn't be a problem moving you to the front of the line."

William let Kat in, and she handed him the syringe. "How long?" she asked.

"Maybe an hour, start to finish. We need to get the residue from inside the syringe and needle. That's not hard to do, but we want to ensure there's no contamination. Did you bring breakfast?"

"No, but I'll buy lunch as soon as we're done," Kat promised.

"What ya thinking, Kat?"

"I have an idea, but I'd rather keep that to myself."

"No problem; let's get started." William pointed to the rack of gowns. "You go gown up and meet me in the lab."

Kat joined William moments later as he was using sterile water to dissolve any residue that might still be inside the syringe. He carefully transferred the contents into a small bottle to be used in the gas chromatograph mass spectrometer. "This will show us different peaks. Each peak represents a different chemical. Won't be too long now. So Captain Moore's wife drowned?"

"Maybe. She was found in the pool, but things just don't add up. Have to wait for the autopsy to know for sure."

"You sure there's going to be an autopsy?" William asked. "Might just do a visual—you know, professional courtesy."

"Oh, there will be an autopsy, especially if these results turn out like I'm thinking they will," Kat replied.

Kat felt the minutes pass like hours. Finally, she could heard the printer engage, and the chart paper started coming out.

"Hmm," William said as he looked at his reference. "Curare. Damn. What's that doing there? That's pretty dangerous stuff. South American natives use it in poisonous darts. It paralyzes the prey within seconds. The animals are still alive, but they can't move. They eventually suffocate from lack of oxygen." William looked up at Kat. "Is that what you were expecting?"

Kat grabbed the results from his hands and headed for the door. "Gotta run, hun. Thanks a million."

"Hey, what about lunch? You promised!"

"Rain check. I promise," Kat called over her shoulder. "This can't wait."

40

Kat had Ric on the phone before she turned the key in her ignition. "Hey, Benny there yet?" she asked.

"Just dropped her off. I'm heading out the door now. Why?" Ric asked.

"I just came from DPS with some lab results that indicate this might not have been an accident. I need you to inspect the body for needle marks. Can you do that before the ME does?"

"Yes, I guess. You think she was using?" Ric asked.

"No, I think someone injected her with curare and let her drown while she was paralyzed."

"Curare? How would someone get access to that in Corpus? That's really dangerous stuff."

"I know. There was a break-in a couple of weeks ago at the veterinary hospital out on Staples. Vet said they broke in to the pharmaceutical closet, and curare was one of the drugs taken."

"Why would the vet have curare?"

"I asked the same question. It seems they use it in cases when a dog or cat is paralyzed by some unknown reason. The curare counteracts whatever is causing the paralysis. The animal is kept alive by artificial respiration until the effects of the curare wears off. He said it's seldom used, but it seems to work really well whenever it's needed."

"Well, that would explain why there was no frothing," Ric said. "Most of the time a drowning victim churns up the water and air in the airway enough to form a white froth. I noticed that there wasn't any there, but I had seen that before. Thought maybe she was just so drunk she passed out and drowned since nobody was there to save her."

"I didn't see a bottle or glass poolside, but I suppose Captain Moore might have cleaned up the scene to save face," Kat said.

"We should know soon enough. I'll draw her blood now and send it off."

"Can you test for curare in the body too?" Kat asked.

"Yes, it's not one of the typical substances we look for. You remember Coppalino versus State?" Ric asked.

"The doctor who killed his neighbor's husband and later his own wife with curare?" Kat said.

"Right. He was having an affair with the neighbor's wife, and they planned to kill off both spouses so they could be together. Trouble was, the good doctor found another woman, and the neighbor's wife ratted him out. Very special case. Curare had never been detected in the human body. It breaks down as it metabolizes, even after death, and doesn't show up on any tests. They had to derive a test to detect the presence of the metabolites, which were there in increased numbers. It actually was a landmark case. The defense argued that the test results shouldn't be allowed since it was not a widely accepted procedure. The judge ruled in favor of the prosecution, stating that new tests would be allowed as long as the science behind the tests was accepted as valid by the scientific community. So to answer your question, kitten, yes. I will make that request."

"When will we know?" Kat asked.

"Tuesday or Wednesday at the earliest."

"Damn. Okay, can we keep this between us for the time being? No need to ruin someone's career if curare is not found in the body."

"Whose career you referring to, kitten?"

Kat laughed half-heartedly. "No comment."

41

Captain Moore took a leave of absence. This immediately caused a conflict within the department, as no one person was in charge, and it seemed that each of the detectives assumed the role, delegating duties to each other and to Kat that they normally would have performed themselves. Kat tried her best to stay above the fray, but she could tell this situation needed to be resolved—and fast. This prompted Kat to set up a meeting with Mayor Rita Montemoya, who had been a successful business person in Corpus Christi for thirty years before going into politics. She was well respected by Republican and Democrats and by whites and Hispanics as well—a feat not easily accomplished in Corpus.

Kat meet with the mayor on Wednesday afternoon and explained that the productivity in her department had fallen off. "I believe if you contact the chief of police, Mayor, and tell him to announce that I'm the interim captain until the situation with Captain Moore is resolved, the other three detectives will accept the chief's decision—even if they don't like it—and everyone could get back to work."

To Kat's surprise, the mayor rebuffed her request. "First," the mayor said, "you can't expect me to tell Chief Gibson to do anything. That man is so stubborn. And second, you have the least experience of all the detectives. What makes you think the chief would place you in charge over the other three?"

"All of them came through the academy at the same time. They won't accept direction from each other. I think because I've solved so many cases, the chief will see me as capable. And to be honest, ma'am, I don't see the chief selecting any of the three others."

"That may very well be the case here, but I refuse to get involved. Chief Gibson will make that determination, and you will just have to accept his decision, as will the other detectives. Now, I'm sorry, but I need to end this meeting. If you will excuse me …" The mayor walked to the door and opened it for Kat.

Kat left without a word. She called Ric on the way back to her office. "Any news?"

"The ME has the lab report. I didn't get to see it. He normally shares, but he's keeping this close to the vest for some reason," said Ric.

"You think that means she was poisoned, maybe with the curare?" Kat asked.

"I think it means he's keeping it close to the vest. That's all I can say at the moment. I'll approach him in a bit, but I can't tell you unless he releases the results. Sorry, kitten."

"Damn. You think he'll cover this up? He and Captain Moore are good friends, aren't they?"

"I can't say what he will or won't do, but I have to believe that no matter what happens, Dr. Elizondo will follow through. He's that kind of man. Dedicated through and through. If it's curare, we'll both know soon enough."

"It's hard to think about anything else," Kat said. "With the captain out of the picture, the other three detectives are bickering about who is in charge. This sucks."

"Hang in there, kitten. Everything has a way of working itself out. You just keep your nose clean, and stay out of the cat fight—no pun intended." Ric chuckled.

"Very funny. Easy for you to say. You don't have to work with those assholes like I do."

"Look, you go home and pop open a cold one, and I will go see Dr. Elizondo. I'll call you tonight if I find out anything."

"Best fuckin' idea I've heard all day," Kat said. "Let me know something either way, okay?"

"Sure thing, kitten. Drink one for me. I'm trying to lose thirty pounds, and my wife won't let me near a beer until I do."

Kat knew that Ric would call later, so she headed for her Mustang, with plans on stopping by the Little Red Barn on her way home. She was out of beer, and that was a quick drive-through; she didn't even have to leave the car.

Kat knocked off the first tallboy before getting halfway home and was feeling a slight buzz as she pulled into the parking lot to her apartment, finished the second, and slid the empty back into the six-pack carton.

"Damn. Doesn't take much to get you drunk on an empty stomach," Kat muttered to herself as she took the remaining four beers upstairs to her apartment.

42

The phone rang around ten, waking Kat where she was dozing on the couch, with both the TV and radio playing. "Hold on, hold on," she said as she hit the remote to silence both electronics. "What's up?"

"Sorry I couldn't call earlier," Ric said. "We got slammed with traffic fatalities. Two dead bodies. Had to draw samples before leaving, and I didn't want to talk at the office. The walls have ears, you know."

"So-o-o-o?" Kat drawled like an Alabama homecoming queen. "What you got for me?"

"You were right; it was curare. The metabolites were five times their normal levels—sure sign of curare."

"What now?"

"ME already called the chief at home. Don't be surprised if you get a call from Dr. Elizondo. The chief asked him to explain the results to you since you are lead on this one."

"Oh great. Break it down for the dumb bitch, huh? That son of a bitch wouldn't know shit about this if it hadn't been for me. Oh well. Thanks, Ric. This really changes things."

"Definitely for you guys; we've done our part. We did notice injection marks, and one of the dieners remembered that Captain Moore asked her to get him syringes last week."

"Oh?" Kat said, unsure whether she should mention that Captain Moore had told her about getting a syringe from the diener.

"Yeah, it could work in his favor, though," Ric said. "I mean, why would he risk asking a diener at the ME's office? He might use that as a defense, saying that if he intended to kill his wife, he could have easily obtained the syringes from a source not connected to law enforcement."

"It could also mean he believed he was too smart to get caught," Kat said.

"Well, the ball is in your court now, kitten. Tread carefully."

"Thanks, Ric. Looks like I'll be paying Captain Moore a call tomorrow. I can't believe this is actually happening; it's so surreal."

Kat hung up the phone but tossed and turned all night. *I have to question the captain again*, she thought. *Only this time it'll be about the* murder *of his wife. And to top it off, I might be placing him under arrest.*

It was not going to be a pleasant day.

43

The phone rang the following morning at the same time her alarm sounded—six o'clock. Kat managed to answer on the fifth ring.

"Detective Gonzales, this is Dr. Elizondo. I have some news that might be instrumental in your investigation of Marlana Moore."

"Yes?" Kay responded, barely awake.

"Her lab work tested positive for the metabolites, indicating that she was injected with curare, a paralyzing poison."

Kat pushed herself to a sitting position and rubbed her temples, trying to clear the sleep from her brain. "You're certain?"

"Curare does not show up as itself. It begins to break down into other chemicals, once its effects have run their course. We test for the other substances. There is more than enough evidence to prove this, so yes, I'm certain. May I continue?"

Kat didn't answer, but the word asshole came to mind.

"We discovered injection sites on her face, as though she was receiving Botox, but there was no sign of Botox in her system. Possibly Mrs. Moore may have trusted the killer enough to allow him or her to give her injections—presumably under the pretense of receiving Botox—but that's more of your element than mine. I thought this information might prove useful."

"Of course," said Kat. "Thank you very much, Doctor. Anything else come to mind?"

"Not at the moment, but I will keep you posted if that changes."

Kat thanked the doctor again before they hung up.

Minutes later, after her shower, she was on the phone with Captain Moore.

"Bob, Kat here. Sorry to have to do this, but could you meet me downtown? I need to go through what happened that night and move on with the investigation. How about the Blue Moon Café in thirty minutes?"

"Make it fifteen," he said curtly. "I want to get this over with. I have funeral arrangements to finalize." He hung up without a goodbye.

The Blue Moon Café was a mainstay in downtown Corpus Christi. It had been serving breakfast, lunch, and dinner since 1957. The grandchildren of the original owners were running things now and trying to modernize by providing free Wi-Fi and offering espresso that was as potent as a caffeine suppository.

Captain Moore was waiting in a booth near the back when Kat walked in. *He probably was already here when I called*, Kat thought. She slid into the booth across from her boss and began without delay. "Can you walk me through Saturday night?"

"Which part?" asked Captain Moore. "The part about the card game or after I got home?"

"All of it, please. I need to establish a timeline."

"Like I said, I was playing cards, like we always do."

Kat interrupted. "What about before the game? What did you do?"

"I had dinner with my wife and left around seven thirty to go to the game."

"Were you drinking?" Kat asked.

"No more than usual, and I always stop in time to allow the effects to dissipate. Wouldn't do for a police captain to get pulled over under the influence, now would it."

"What time did you leave the game?"

"Like I told you before, at ten thirty."

"The others can verify that?"

"Of course they can. We went through this already. What's going on?"

"Bear with me, please," Kat said. "What time did you arrive home?"

The captain rolled his eyes. "At eleven."

"And did you see your wife at that time?"

"No. I didn't see her until I found her the next morning."

"Was she expecting company while you played cards?"

"Not to my knowledge. She was excited about something, but would not let on what it was."

"Did your wife ever mention getting Botox injections?"

"Good Lord, no. Why would she do that?"

"You'd be surprised," Kat replied.

"What's going on? Do you have information you aren't telling me?"

"Injection marks were discovered on your wife's face," Kat said. "There were in the same locations as for someone receiving Botox injections. It's possible that someone may have poisoned Marlana under the pretense of giving her Botox."

"Poisoned? How?" he asked. "With what?"

"Curare," Kat said. "The autopsy indicates that Marlana had curare in her system. That could explain why there was no frothing as she drowned. It would have paralyzed her, and she would not have been able to move to prevent her drowning."

"Good God," he said. "You're positive?"

"About the curare, yes. The means of getting it into her is conjecture at the moment."

With that, Kat stood up, looked down at her captain, and walked out of the Blue Moon. She drove straight to the ME's office; she needed to talk with Marissa.

The diener confirmed that Captain Moore had indeed stopped by on Friday afternoon to pick up some syringes.

"You said *some.* How many did he get?" Kat asked.

"Two, I believe," said Marissa.

"It's important that I know exactly."

She nodded. "Yes. Two. I saw him pick up two from the drawer over there by the scales; that's where we keep them."

"You're positive?"

"Yes."

"Okay, thanks. I'll be in touch." Kat exited the building.

On her drive to the police station, Kat played out in her head why Captain Moore would say he only picked up one syringe when the diener saw him get two. *If you're getting a syringe, why lie about how many?*

At the station Kat went immediately to the fourth floor, the Forensics lab. The ID techs had just returned, so Kat asked, "Did either of you find another syringe?"

"No," said the tech. "Why?"

"Just checking. Thanks."

Kat went to her computer and began typing out a search warrant for her captain's vehicles. "Now which judge will sign this?" Kat thought aloud. "Velma. Velma Herrera. She and Bob have crossed paths several times, and neither likes the other."

Judge Herrera was more than happy to sign the warrant giving Kat permission to search Captain Moore's cruiser and Marlana's vehicle as well.

Kat contacted ID. "I need Joel to meet me at 236 Oleander in fifteen minutes."

Kat liked Joel. He was in some of the entomology classes she had taken from Roxanne.

"What's this about?" Joel asked when he arrived at Captain Moore's residence.

"We are looking for a syringe, so be careful," Kat said.

Joel knew better than to ask why; that was one reason Kat wanted him here. He was professional and had a solid reputation among the other police officers, even though he was just a civilian—the Corpus PD did not use officers as ID techs. Even better, all the judges in town knew and respected his work.

After Moore's cruiser turned up blank, Kat said, "Okay, now to the wife's car."

"What makes you think there's a syringe in her vehicle?" Joel asked.

"Captain Moore picked up two from the ME's office, but we located only one syringe. Nothing on the grounds or in the trash. Just trying to track down a possible lead."

"This is Moore's house? Geez, I knew the cruiser was PD, but I had no idea. The other techs worked the scene. What's the scoop?"

"Can't really say," Kat replied. "Maybe the missing syringe can clear that up."

"Well, get ready to see things a little clearer," Joel said with a broad grin. "Lookie what I found under the driver's seat." He produced an almost empty syringe.

"Great bag and tag," said Kat "And let's get it over to DPS to find out what's inside."

"Done and done. You coming?" Joel asked.

"Be there in a few. I have other pressing matters that need some attention first. Call me as soon as you know, if I'm not there."

Kat headed to the ME's office. She called Ric on the way. "You see any other injection sites on Marlana Moore besides those on her face?"

"No, but the water had wrinkled her flesh. Could be one we missed."

"Would you mind prepping her again? I need to check out something. I'll fill you in when I arrive."

"You got it, kitten."

The deceased bodies were kept covered in a refrigerated room on a rolling plastic gurney. ("Refrigerated, not frozen" she'd heard Ric say dozens of times as college classes toured the facility.) Once the body was placed on the gurney, it remained there until it was picked up by a funeral home. Dr. Elizondo performed his examinations in one of two rooms. The head end of the gurney was slightly higher than the foot, which had a hole that was placed above the sink for the blood to drain. This type of setup made it possible for smaller individuals, like Marissa, to roll the bodies wherever they were needed.

After Kat was buzzed through the outer office, she crossed the small open atrium and entered the portion of the building where the evidence was stored—bodies, tissue samples, suicide notes, even autoerotic asphyxiation apparatus.

Ric had the body in the examination room. "What are we looking for?" he asked.

"We found two syringes. I want to see if there's an injection site on the arms or hip region."

"I can tell you there's nothing on her hips, but the arms were difficult to exam due to the pruning caused by the water."

Seeing no Y incision on the chest, Kat seemed disappointed. "No autopsy?"

"Not yet," said Ric. "May not be one. It's up to the doctor to decide."

Without delay, Kat and Ric began searching the body for the telltale sign of a needle mark.

"Got it," Kat said after about five minutes.

"Let me see." Ric slid over to the side Kat was on. A small puncture could be seen on the left tricep. "Sure is. Good eye. What's next?"

"Waiting to see what's in the second syringe. I'm headed to DPS now."

"Keep me posted, kitten."

"Always, Ric. It may not be the doctor's decision after all. We'll see."

Kat's phone beeped as she headed to her car. "Joel, what you got?"

"Demerol. There was almost two CCs left in the syringe. No way to tell how much was there originally."

"Thanks, Joel. Good work. Let's keep this between us for now. I've got some questions that need answering before we go too far on this."

"You got it."

She went back inside the ME's office, where she found Ric moving the body back into the cooler.

"How much Demerol would it take to sedate a woman of her size?" Kat asked, pointing at their captain's deceased wife.

"Depends. If alcohol also was ingested, maybe .25 milligrams per pound; otherwise .5 milligrams per pound of body weight should make her drowsy enough to lose consciousness. That's what was in the other syringe?"

"Exactly. Will you inform Dr. Elizondo?"

"Certainly. I'm sure that will prompt him to perform a full autopsy now."

"Let's hope so." Once again, Kat exited the building.

Kat wanted to head straight to Chief Gibson's office to inform him of everything that had transpired over the last few days, but she held off. *I need the results from the autopsy*, she thought. *Patience. This isn't* CSI Las Vegas, *where you solve every case in an hour.*

She had other investigations pending, and as much as she dreaded going into the office, that's where she was headed. "Those SOBs better not say one word to me about Moore."

Kat slid into her cubicle unnoticed by the other three detectives, who still were bickering about who should be in charge.

It wasn't long before Detective Aguilar stopped by her desk. "Where do you stand on Marlana?" he asked. "Accidental drowning? Suicide?"

"I can't discuss it right now, Augie. Catch you later, please?"

"You find something? What? I'd tell you."

"I'm sure you would, but I've got other cases screaming at me. Now if you don't mind, I'm just trying to do my job here."

"We all are, doll." And with that, Detective Javier Aguilar disappeared from her view.

Two minutes later, Detectives Timms and Huerta were sitting on either end of Kat's desk, with her sandwiched in between.

"We are all cops here," said Jacob Huerta. "What's going on?"

"Obliviously no police work, as far as I can see," Kat retorted. "Don't you fellas have cases to work? If not, then I can send some of mine your way." Kat stood and without saying goodbye, she left the building and went to City Hall. She didn't have an appointment with the mayor, but with the information Kat was holding, she figured the mayor would see her.

Halfway there, Kat reevaluated her position. "Damn. I need the autopsy results. Even if he did it today, it would still take another twenty-four hours to get the labs back."

Kat looked at the folders she was carrying in her briefcase. An incident had happened the night before. A police car had been involved with another vehicle around eleven thirty. The driver of the other vehicle pulled out in front of the cruiser. The driver insisted that the police car was driving with its lights off.

Kat headed back to the station. Not wanting to run into coworkers on the elevator, she used the stairs to go the four flights to reach ID.

Kat signed out the large brown paper bag containing the broken headlight from the police cruiser. The filament was intact and not burned. This indicated to Kat that the lights indeed had been off when the accident occurred. She knew that the filament would have been burned completely, had the lens broken, allowing air to rush in while the hot filament was lit.

"Damn. Chief warned us about driving through neighborhoods without using headlights," Kat said loud enough for Joel to hear. "He's not going to like this."

Joel came closer. "You know we caught those kids who broke into the vet's office and stole all those drugs. They thought they could make some money dealing."

"First I've heard," Kat said.

"Anyway, guess whose signature is on the evidence log, checking out the stash."

"No way."

"Yes, way—Captain Robert Moore."

"Is anything missing? Curare? Demerol?" Kat asked.

"All vials are accounted for, but there's no way to tell if somebody used a syringe to draw out samples," Joel replied.

"And the shit keeps getting deeper," Kat said and then bit her lip at letting that slip. "I ... uh, have to see the chief about the incident last night."

"Which incident?" Joel asked.

"The one involving the patrol officer hitting the civilian's vehicle. See ya."

Kat took the elevator to Chief Gibson's floor. She didn't care who she ran into; she was on a mission.

Juanita, Chief Gibson's administrative assistant, informed Kat that she should make an appointment to see the chief. "He's a very busy man," she said. "As a matter of fact, the mayor is in there now."

Kat seized the opportunity. "I can kill two birds with one stone," she said as she blew past Juanita.

"Or end a career," Juanita retorted.

Kat thrust the door open and could tell immediately that she was interrupting something personal between the two. The mayor started to leave, but Kat stopped her. "You should hear this too, Mayor." Kat decided to go for it all, knowing the next few minutes could make or break her career. "Some developments have unfolded in the Marlana Moore case."

Chief Gibson scowled at her. "And you couldn't *call* to tell me that? You come busting down my door, interrupting an important meeting between the mayor and me. There better be some damn important developments, Detective Gonzales."

"They are, sir." Kat proceeded to inform them of the two syringes' contents and that Captain Moore had access to those substances in the crime lab.

"You are risking the reputation of an officer with over thirty years' experience and that of this department over the contents of two syringes. The media would love that, wouldn't they. I understand that you think you have a smoking gun here, but too much is at stake. You have to be certain before you go spouting off about something like this."

"We could be certain, sir, if the ME would just do his job," Kat replied.

"Dismissed, Gonzales."

Kat fought back tears as she walked past Juanita.

She had ruined her chance of a promotion, and the thought of any one of those bozo detectives becoming her boss was too much for one day.

Her Mustang could have driven to Alice on autopilot. Kat hit the cruise control and let her mind wander. It had been too long since she'd had her mom's chicken tortilla soup.

Before she broke free of the Corpus city limits, Kat's phone beeped. She hit the hands-free button on her dash. "Hola."

"What's my favorite kitten up to these days?" Roxanne asked.

"Headed to Alice."

Roxanne could read her tone of voice, even over the phone. "Uh-oh. What's going on?"

Kat laughed. "You know me too well. How 'bout I pick up some brisket and ribs and then tell you up close and personal? I know, I know, 'Don't forget the beer.' I do need something stronger than soup."

"Well, in that case, forget the beer. I've got a couple of bottles of wine I wouldn't mind sharing."

Kat's Mustang veered left instead of right and headed directly to Roxanne's. *This is just what I need*, she thought as the Mustang gained speed.

Over the first bottle of J. Lohr cabernet, Kat laid out what had been taking place with her investigation of Marlana Moore's death.

"You think Moore did it?" Roxanne asked.

"I hate to say it, but …"

"But nothing. What?"

"The evidence points his way," Kat replied.

"Answer the question I asked," Roxanne said as she poured Kat a glass from bottle number two.

"Yes," Kat admitted. "Yes, I believe Captain Moore drugged his wife with Demerol, carried her drowsy body to the pool, injected her face with curare to make the injection site appear to be Botox, and then let Marlana drown without her putting up a fight. That's how I see it."

"Wowzers, kitten. Can you prove that?"

"Not without the autopsy report," Kat said.

"Even then, how can you place Moore as being the one giving the injections?"

"I can't—not yet anyway."

"Well then, doll, you'd better drink up 'cause nothing else is gonna happen tonight—at least not with your case anyway."

"No, no way. I'm not going out tonight. Not after two bottles," Kat said.

"Who said anything about stopping at two bottles?" Roxanne laughed.

"I have to go in after lunch tomorrow. Mind if I crash here tonight?" Kat asked.

"Mi casa es tu casa," Roxanne said as they both took another long drink.

45

Hungover and hungry, Kat was on her way to the police station when her phone beeped. She answered with, "I didn't say goodbye because you were still asleep."

The silence on the other end told Kat that she was not on the phone with Roxanne.

The caller cleared his throat and then said, "I'm not exactly sure what that implies, nor do I wish to know, Detective Gonzales, but I do have some pertinent information regarding your investigation of Marlana Moore's death. Lab reports also show Demerol was in her system. I'm planning to open her up this afternoon and conduct a very thorough autopsy. I'll keep you posted on what I find." Dr. Elizondo hung up.

Kat was embarrassed but at the same time elated. *Now, how can I prove that Captain Moore injected Marlana?*

46

All eyes turned toward Kat as she made her way to her desk, but she intentionally kept her head low, making no eye contact and trying to give the appearance of being consumed with her work. *Maybe they will take the hint*, she thought.

No such chance.

"I hear they are going to cut Marlana today," Detective Timms said matter-of-factly.

"How would you know that?" Kat asked.

"Oh, we know. Nothing happens around here that we don't already know or find out about as soon as it occurs." Timms smiled.

"Well, then, maybe you should use some of that magic and solve some of those cases in the folders on your desk. If you will excuse me, I have some urgent business that needs my immediate attention." Kat stood up and left the room.

She headed for the ladies room as fast as she could manage without breaking into a full sprint. Once inside, she hurried to the first stall and purged about half a bottle of red wine. "Tasted a lot better last night," she muttered. "Damn. Everybody knows my business about as fast as I do."

Her phone rang; it was Joel from ID.

"Hey, Kat, I overheard Brenda talking to Moore. She worked the scene, and she collected the dirty clothes from the hamper. She's going to give Captain Moore his clothes back since she didn't find any evidence. I think she has a thing for Captain Moore, hence the special treatment."

"Holy shit! I can't believe she is going to do that. I'll be there in five minutes."

Kat hit the button on the elevator to go up to ID. She walked in and addressed Brenda Lopez without preamble. "I'd like to take a look at the clothing from the Moore residence. Let's use the alternate light source."

Brenda handed Kat the filtered goggles, turned on the alternate light source to seven hundred nanometers, and cut off the overhead light. All the clothing from Captain Moore and Marlana Moore were laid out, and the red beam of light went over each garment. Brenda then adjusted the ALS to 570 nanometers, which produced a yellow light, and the process was repeated.

Kat saw a luminous spot on the bottom of one of Captain Moore's T-shirts. "What's that?"

"Not sure," Brenda replied. "I went over with it with a magnifying glass, but I didn't see it under natural light."

"Let's take a sample of it right now and then continue with the ALS," Kat said.

Brenda adjusted the ALS to a lower wavelength. On another portion of the same garment, they both saw a trail of illuminated spots.

"I'll grab some of those samples," said Brenda

After twenty more minutes with the ALS, without finding any more evidence, Kat turned on the overhead light.

"Let's get those samples to DPS right away," Kat said.

"Captain Moore is coming to pick up his and Marlana's clothing," Brenda said.

"Don't alert him. This could turn out to be nothing. Give him back everything but his T-shirt. Maybe he won't miss it. You stay here and give him his clothes. I'll run the samples over to DPS."

As soon as Kat was out of the police building, she hit her speed dial to call William at DPS. "Hey, I have another favor to ask."

"These favors seem to only run one way. Why is that?" William asked.

She laughed. "I don't know. What can I do for you?"

"Nothing. Just tell me what you need this time."

"I have two more samples I need you to run, and let's just keep the findings between you and me for right now."

"I'm seeing a pattern here. Am I your own personal laboratory slave?"

"No, no, no—nothing like that. I just don't want to cause any alarms to go off if this turns out to be nothing. How about I treat you to dinner afterward?"

"Oh yeah, right. I'm sure my wife would really appreciate me going out to dinner with someone who looks like you. Just get your ass over here. Everybody is on their way out, and I'll run the samples."

47

The results of the first sample came back as Demerol. The second turned out to be curare. Kat looked at the results with amazement.

"Holy shit-wad."

"You really need to work on your descriptions there, kitten," William said. "What does this mean to you?"

"This means everything! I need you to have these tests recorded as viable evidence in the case of Marlana Moore's death. I think it is safe to say it is a homicide. Can you fax these results over to the DA? I'm headed to the chief's office."

48

Kat called Juanita, the chief's secretary, and requested a meeting with the chief, ASAP. "I have important information that the chief will want to know."

Juanita sighed heavily, clearly displeased, but she said, "I'll inform the chief."

Kat then called Brenda from ID and asked if Captain Moore had picked up the clothing.

"Yes, but he didn't say anything about the T-shirt," Brenda said.

"Good, good," said Kat. "I need for you to meet me at the chief's office in ten minutes."

"Why is that?"

"Because you are going to tell that fat bastard what we found on Captain Moore's T-shirt."

"You got the results back already?" asked Brenda. "What was on the T-shirt?

"Demerol and curare."

"Holy … holy smokes! Both of those were found in Marlana's system. The walls have ears here, you know."

"Yeah, I know."

49

Brenda was sitting on a couch across from Juanita when Kat entered the room. Juanita looked up and said, "Go in. He's waiting on you."

Brenda grimaced at Kat. "I wasn't going in there alone."

"You just tell him what you found," Kat said.

They entered Chief Gibson's office and took the seats that were offered in front of his desk. "Well?" the chief asked.

Kat looked at Brenda and nodded her encouragement.

Brenda sat up a little straighter as she addressed the chief. "Chief, we gathered clothing from the Moore residence. While looking at the evidence under ALS, we discovered traces of two different chemicals. Detective Gonzales has the results of our findings."

Kat leveled her eyes at the chief. "One of the samples is Demerol, and the other proved to be curare."

Chief Gibson pursed his lips. "This came from where?"

"From a T-shirt I gathered from Captain Moore's dirty clothes hamper," said Brenda.

"This is big. You're certain it came from Captain Moore's T-shirt and not his wife's?"

"Well, it was an extra-large Texas A&M T-shirt—much too big for Marlana," Brenda explained. "Besides, everyone knows Marlana was a huge UT fan. Oh, and it came from the clothes hamper in Captain Moore's bedroom."

"I see," said the chief. "Good work. Now if you will excuse us, Ms. Lopez, I need to speak with Detective Gonzales." After Brenda had left the room, the chief turned to Kat. "So, Detective, it looks like you got your smoking gun. You'll inform the DA's office of your findings and turn the case over to them. I hope you crossed all your t's and dotted all your i's. Looks like I'm going to have to assign somebody to take over Captain Moore's position. Who would you suggest?"

Without hesitation, Kat said, "Me. I'm the only one who is not part of the good ole boys. Over the last two years I've solved more cases than the other three detectives combined."

"I kind of figured you might say that," the chief said as he stood up. "Thank you."

Kat took her cue, rose, and left the room. She didn't go back to her office; instead, she hopped in her Mustang and pointed it toward Alice. She needed more time to think.

The next morning Kat awoke in her childhood bedroom. She walked into the kitchen to the aroma of her father's coffee and her mother frying bacon. She sat down across the table from her father as her mother served her a cup of strong coffee, just the way her father liked it.

"Sleep well, mija?" her father asked.

"Yes, thanks."

"To what do we owe the pleasure of your visit?" he continued.

"I just needed some time away, and I wanted to see you two. It's been too long."

Standing over the stove, her mother said, "You didn't bring any bags. Aren't you staying?"

"No, I'm sorry. I can't. I just didn't want to be alone last night."

"Well, you know Ms. Sylvia's son, Roel, is getting a divorce. You two used to be together all the time in high school."

"So you are playing matchmaker, huh?" her father said. "Our daughter has come here to relax, and you are trying to fix her up. Mind your own business, *querida*."

Kat's mom turned the strips of bacon and asked, "Pancakes?"

"No, Mama. Thank you. I'll try a couple of slices of bacon before I go."

"Sí, the usual," said her father.

Kat watched as her dad ate three pancakes as she nibbled on two slices of bacon. Her mother had yet to sit down at the table. Kat smiled at her parents. *I'm glad they are in the dark about what's going on*, she thought. *They are such nice people.* She walked over to the stove and wrapped her arms around her mother. She kissed her on the back of her neck and said, "I love you, Mama." Then she hugged her dad tightly and whispered in his ear, "I love you, Papa."

He kissed her cheek just before she pulled away and walked out the door, fighting back tears.

She was in her Mustang, headed back to Corpus, when she got a call from the secretary at the DA's office.

"The district attorney would like to speak with you at nine o'clock."

"You'd better make it ten. I'm not in town, but I can get there by ten o'clock."

So much for a little peace and quiet. Let the show begin.

Once in town, Kat hurried to her apartment, showered, dressed, and made it to the DA's office with five minutes to spare, even though her hair was still wet. She was ushered into a room with a large table, around which were faces she recognized—the assistant DAs and with District Attorney Rolando Valadez seated at the head of the table. Kat could sense she was interrupting a heated discussion as everyone rose to greet her.

DA Valadez extended his arm and pointed at a seat at the far end of the table. "Please be seated, Detective Gonzales, and tell us what you know about the death of Marlana Moore."

Kat went step by step, from the moment she received the call from the chief to come to Captain Moore's residence, to their finding traces of Demerol and curare in Marlana's system, to finally discovering the Demerol and curare on Captain Moore's T-shirt. DA Valadez remained silent, but some of the assistant DAs asked questions. *Unimportant questions,* Kat thought, but she answered them nonetheless.

When she'd finished, Rolando Valadez commended her on her thoroughness and said, "I know this must be hard on you to be investigating your own boss. We both have our work cut out for us. Keep up the good job."

"Thank you," Kat said and left about as fast as she'd come.

There were a hundred other places she would rather have gone, but she went to her office anyway. She was relieved to find it empty. *I guess those other SOBs finally got off their asses to do something.* She didn't know that the other three detectives were in Chief Gibson's office. The chief was filling them in on the particulars of the Moore case and Marlana's homicide.

"Captain Moore will remain on leave of absence," the chief said. "I will be assigning one of you to serve as interim captain as soon as this situation is resolved."

The three detectives returned to their office and were surprised to see Kat sitting at her desk.

Javier spoke first. "Chief informed us what's going on with the investigation of Captain Moore. I hate to say it, but that is pretty damn good police work, Detective Gonzales."

Timms said, "I can't believe Captain Moore would do that."

"Believe what you want," Kat said indifferently. "The evidence speaks for itself."

Huerta chimed in. "It looks like one of us will be acting captain."

"What makes you say that?" Kat asked.

"The chief said one of us three will be assigned as interim captain."

Kat looked him in the eyes and said, "He specifically said one of you three will be serving as captain?"

Aguilar, Huerta, and Timms all nodded in agreement.

Kat forced a smile in utter disbelief without saying a word.

51

Kat's first instinct was to call Roxanne, but she resisted. Roxanne would tell her that Aguilar probably would serve as captain because of his experience. She knew that was probably right, but Kat had always pulled for the underdog. This time, *she* was the underdog.

She picked up a folder and turned her attention toward the twenty-five-year-old white male who had left a gentlemen's club called Titti Citi and tried to cross the eight lanes of South Padre Island Drive on foot. Toxicology reports showed his blood alcohol content was 0.28.

How was he even walking? Kat thought. The victim's family was suing Titti Citi for overserving their son. *Why is this case even on my desk? Never mind. I need something like this to get my mind off everything.* She headed out the door to speak with the manager at the strip club.

When she got there, the club was still closed, and the manager was nowhere to be found. Kat drove out to the beach to contemplate what was going to happen at her office. She couldn't imagine working for any of those three. Not even one of them came close to being like Captain Moore.

She was the most logical choice, but that was not going to happen. Her thoughts were interrupted by the sound of her phone. It was the manager of Titti Citi returning her call. He agreed to meet Kat at the club before it opened up for the evening. He also said he would have the bartender and waitresses who worked that night come in as well.

"Perfect!" she said into the phone, but *perfuck* is what she thought as she headed toward the strip club.

Titti Citi's bartender told Kat, "The victim's bill showed only two shots of Patron. No one gets that drunk on two shots."

One of the waitresses spoke up. "I saw him slip a bottle into his boot."

"What kind of bottle?" Kat asked.

"A flat bottle with a black label. Something like Jack Daniel's. I was busy serving drinks and didn't say anything. Next thing I knew, he was gone."

Another waitress spoke up. "I saw him head toward the men's room."

"He went out through the emergency exit by the men's room. The alarms are faulty, so it didn't make any sound. If he had walked out the front door, we would have stopped him," said the manager.

"I'm sure of it. Did anyone see anything else?" Kat scanned each of their eyes.

"We are sorry this happened, but we didn't do anything wrong," the manager insisted. "We didn't know the guy snuck in his own bottle. That is strictly against policy here. Hell, it's against Texas Alcoholic Beverage Commission law."

"Got it," Kat said as she stood. "Thank you for coming in."

Kat's phone rang at three thirty in the morning. She was still awake.

It was Chief Gibson. "Sorry to call you in the middle of the night. There's been a shooting down on the beach, a mile or so from Bob Hall Pier. Officers involved. Get there as soon as you can."

"Roger that," said Kat.

Five minutes later she was in her Mustang, and twenty minutes later she arrived at the scene. It was still dark, but with all the blue lights flashing, the area was lit up like a Smurf's Christmas. Detective Aguilar spotted her right away and met her as she was getting out of her car.

"I can't believe it," he said. "Timms and Huerta—they are both dead."

"*What?* How?" Kat asked as she exited her car.

"Gunshots. Looks like they shot *each other* at close range. I got a text from Huerta, telling me to come here, to this spot. When I arrived, I saw the car in the water with the driver's side door open. Moments later, I received gunfire from the dunes. I returned fire. Officers are searching the dunes, but they haven't turned up anything yet."

"What did you do next?" Kat asked.

"I went to the car to check for signs of life. I could tell by their wounds that they were both dead. Both shot in the head. I then called dispatch and tried to keep the car from floating out into the Gulf—it was filling up as the tide was rising. I attached a rope to their cruiser and pulled it onto the beach using my vehicle."

"What do you think happened?" Kat asked.

"I don't know. We all wanted to be captain. Maybe those two got in an argument that escalated and got violent."

"They would kill each other over a job?" Kat asked.

"Alcohol may be involved. I don't know. We'll have to wait for the tox screen."

Moments later, Kat saw the ID van pull up behind her Mustang. Joel came out the passenger side.

"Working late tonight," Kat called to him.

"Yeah, that's why they pay us the big bucks," Joel said. He opened the back of the van so he and Brenda could get their crime scene cases.

"Okay, what do we got here?" Brenda asked Kat.

"Detective Aguilar was first on the scene and discharged his weapon, so I'll let him fill you in as you swab his hands for gunshot residue. I'm going to go take a look at the vehicle."

"Not before me," Joel said. "You cops are the worst. I need to photograph the scene before you set one foot near it."

Kat turned sideways and pointed Joel toward the scene; then she followed at a distance, letting him do his job. Joel photographed the entire outside of the vehicle, opened the doors, and photographed the inside. Kat could see Timms slumped over the steering wheel and Huerta sitting upright in the passenger side. *Not a pretty sight.*

She scanned the sand for any other traces of evidence. She expelled a sigh of relief when she failed to locate any tire marks or footprints, other than those made by Detective Aguilar as he pulled the vehicle from the water.

Javier approached Kat. "What are you looking for?"

"Any trace of someone else having been here."

"You think someone else shot them?" Javier asked.

"No, I'm not saying that. I'm just looking to see if we have a missing third party."

"There was definitely someone else around 'cause someone fired at me," Javier said.

"Did you see where the bullets hit or hear them go by you?"

"No, I just heard the gunfire. It came from the dunes, so I returned fire. I assumed someone was shooting at me."

Kat looked up into the dunes and saw a flashlight surveying the land. "That's where the shots came from?" Kat asked, pointing at the direction of the flashlight. "Let's go check it out. Once the sun's up, we need to do a thorough search of this area, all the way out to the road."

Javier nodded. "Let's make sure they're not still out there."

As Kat and Javier surveyed the area, they could see at least a dozen flashlights.

"It looks like they got that covered," Kat said. "Let's go back to the car."

Joel was just finishing his rough sketch of the scene as they approached. He pointed toward the car and said, "Ric is around front."

Kat approached Ric. "What are you doing?"

"Just looking at the position of the bodies before I look in the vehicles," he answered, "and jotting down notes. Tell me what you see."

"I see two dead coworkers."

"Is that all?"

"Well, I see Detective Timms with a gunshot wound to his head, slumped over the steering wheel. I see Detective Huerta, also with a gunshot wound to his head, on the passenger side."

"What do you notice about the angles of their bodies?"

"Hmm … it doesn't really match the scenario laid out by Detective Aguilar."

"How so?"

"Well, if they had shot each other, the bodies would have been positioned more toward the sides of the vehicle, not upright like they are."

"Anything else?" Ric asked.

"Yes, the blood spatter would be on the sides as well. It would be on the side glass rather than the windshield," Kat said. "Are there exit wounds?"

"I'm done here. Let's go see."

Ric slowly opened the passenger door where Detective Huerta's body sat. He began to dictate into his handheld tape recorder. "Appears to be gunshot to the front passenger victim, Detective Huerta, that entered near the left temporal lobe. No exit wound noticed at this time. Blood spatter from victim appears on the headliner upholstery overhead and on the front side of the windshield. It appears that Huerta was facing forward in the vehicle when he was shot. We will know more when we get the body back for an autopsy."

Leaving the passenger door open, Ric and Kat walk over to the driver's side. Ric began again. "There appears to be a hole in the roof of the vehicle, possibly made by a bullet." Ric opened the driver's side door. "The driver has entrance and exit wounds to the head. I don't want to speculate because the exit wound is not always larger than the entry wound, but it does appear that the driver, Detective Timms, was shot just behind the right ear, with the bullet possibly exiting the top of the forehead over the left eye."

Ric shut off his tape recorder. He pulled a small knife from his kit and made a small puncture in the abdominal cavity, just large enough to insert a thermometer. He then walked over and repeated the process on the other victim. He waited several minutes and took readings from both thermometers, jotting them down in his notepad.

"What did you get?" Kat asked

"No sign of livor mortis, and rigor has yet to set in. Algor mortis indicate they're been dead for two hours, possible three."

"Well, that goes along with what Detective Aguilar was saying, time-wise. I just think he is wrong about what transpired."

"Benny should be here shortly," Ric said. "We'll get the bodies transported back to the ME's office. Dr. Elizondo will perform the autopsies as soon as he arrives this morning."

54

K-9 units arrived on the scene just as the sun was rising over the Gulf of Mexico.

Kat looked out over the water and took in the brilliance of the sun reflecting off the Gulf. *I need to take in more sunrises*, she thought, *but not like this*. She turned to head toward the dunes and sighed. *Two hours and no telling how many square miles turned up absolutely nothing. No spent cartridges, no torn clothing, no footprints, except those made by the officers doing the initial search.*

Detective Aguilar approached.

"We got nothing," she said as she scanned Javier's face for his response.

"Well, I know what I heard and saw. Someone was here in the dunes and fired three shots. I returned fire, and the shooting stopped."

"Since you are involved, it looks like I'll be leading the investigation."

"Bullshit. I was here first. I'll be conducting the investigation."

Kat walked over to her Mustang, got behind the wheel, and managed to find a path out to the road. She was looking forward to catching up on a little sleep. *Like that's going to happen*, she thought. *I can't believe that dipshit wants the lead on this. Wait, yes I can. That is exactly his MO.*

Kat growled in frustration and then began talking to herself out loud, debating both sides of her argument, as if she had multiple personalities. "Okay, let him run with this. Let him fuck it up. It just puts you in the driver's seat once the chief realizes what a screwup he actually is. Yes, but these are fellow officers, and they are dead. They deserve better, even though they were assholes. Okay, okay, just let it rest. Remember the Serenity Prayer. I know, I know, but I can fix this."

Kat went back to her apartment, showered, made a pot of coffee, and started dressing for the day.

The phone rang, and although the caller started speaking without identifying himself, she recognized the voice of Chief Gibson.

"I've heard the news. I want you to take over the cases that Timms and Huerta were working. I've been in contact with the Texas Rangers. They'll be sending two of their personnel to Corpus to help out until we can replace the detectives we just lost. One is from Houston; the other is from Austin. Make sure they get up to speed when they get here tomorrow. In the meantime, I trust you know what to do."

"Who is going to investigate this shooting?" Kat asked.

"Detective Aguilar and I have spoken this morning. He was first on the scene. He will conduct the investigation."

Kat wanted to tell the chief what she and Ric had discovered, but she thought better of it. Instead, she said "Thank you" and hung up the phone.

Well, fuck me to the moon and back! Now I have two more pricks to deal with on top of Javier royally fucking up the investigation. This is really too bad to be true.

The building was quiet when she arrived. *Word spreads fast*, she thought as she took the stairs. She didn't want to be trapped in an elevator with other police officers asking what happened. Once in the office, she looked at the empty desks of Timms and Huerta.

"Slobs," she said out loud as she surveyed their messy desktops. She went to Timms's desk and began stacking folders to get some sense of organization. She placed the stack on her own desk and repeated the process for Huerta's cases. She then prioritized them, giving her a place to start.

"I'll give these two new hotshots the bottom of the pile," she said.

Just then, Detective Aguilar came through the door. Clearly he had not taken the time to go home and change clothes. He still had sand on his shoes.

"I'm headed to the ME's office," he said. "I'm going to be there for the autopsies." He left without saying another word.

Kat opened the top folder and read about a Mrs. Brown, a forty-eight-year-old married female, mother of two, reported missing by her sister. She called the phone number listed by the sister, who answered on the first ring. Kat identified herself as Detective Gonzales from the CCPD and informed Ms. Olivarez, Mrs. Brown's sister, that she would be taking over the investigation.

"Good. That other guy never called me back. I left several messages."

Ignoring that, Kat said, "So the last time you talked to your sister was five days ago? The notes indicate you talk with her on a daily basis. Have there been other occasions when you haven't spoken with your sister over an extended time?"

"Yes, she has taken off a couple of times, but only for two or three days at a time."

"When was the last time that occurred?"

"It's been over a year. I told that to the other detective."

"I understand. I'm just verifying information here. I'm going to speak with Mr. Brown, and then I'll come by to visit with you later."

"My kids get out of school at three. Can you come before then? I don't want them to hear us talking about their auntie. They are very close to her."

"I'll touch base with you as soon as I can." Without hanging up the receiver, Kat pushed the button to end the call and immediately dialed Mr. Brown's number.

Several rings later, she heard a gruff voice on the other end of the line. "Yeah, who is this?"

Kat explained who she was and asked if they could meet later that morning.

Mr. Brown didn't ask why Kat wanted to meet. He only said he would be available after eleven o'clock.

Kat wanted to have Mr. Brown come to the police station, but with all the turmoil, she thought it best to meet at his residence.

Besides, that would give her a chance to look around. Kat looked at the folder again and she said, "That's 202 Bradshaw at eleven this morning."

"*After* eleven," came the reply.

56

Kat sat back in her chair and reflected on what had occurred at the beach that morning. *If the autopsy points toward a third shooter, where and who could that have been? From the back seat? What about the gunfire from the dunes? The only person to witness that was Javier. There is no sign of anyone having been in the dunes. Javier is hell-bent on insisting those two shot each other. What if he was the one in the back seat? If I was the DA, what would be my take on this? I would need evidence left by the shooter.*

Kat could hardly wait to hear back from Ric. She needed those autopsy reports. She wondered what Javier would say once they dispelled his theory. Kat wanted another cup of coffee and a chocolate-covered doughnut before she met with Mr. Brown. She needed to keep her energy up.

She arrived at 202 Bradshaw at 11:05. She knocked on the door. No answer. She decided to wait in her Mustang for Mr. Brown to arrive home. Ten minutes later, a blue Chevy pickup pulled into the drive. A white male—she guessed he was about six foot two—wearing all white, with traces of about a hundred different colors of paint covering his clothes, top to bottom, emerged from the truck.

So he is a painter, Kat thought and then smiled. *I went to detective school to figure that out, Captain Obvious.* The man she assumed was Mr. Brown walked straight into the house before Kat could exit her vehicle. She knocked on the door, and moments later the door opened.

The man asked without a greeting, "Is this going to take long? I have to get back to work."

"Hopefully not. I'm Detective Gonzales, by the way."

"What happened to Timmy?" the man asked, not really seeming to care.

"If you are referring to Detective Timms, he is no longer working this case."

"Did he get fired?"

He kinda did, Kat thought. But aloud, she said, "No. Are you Mr. Brown?"

"Yes." He opened the screen door and stepped aside so Kat could enter the house.

Kat noticed a pungent odor as she crossed over the threshold. She knew that Mrs. Brown had been gone for almost a week. Clothes lay on the floor, and remnants of TV dinners were stacked high on the end tables.

Kat looked for a place to sit down, even though Mr. Brown hadn't offered. Facing Mr. Brown, she said, "You told Detective Timms you last saw your wife five days ago, but you did not report her missing."

"Her sister did."

"Why is that?" Kat asked.

"Judith has taken off before, but she always comes back. I guess it's taken her a longer time to come back this time. I didn't want to make a big deal out of nothing."

"What was your conversation like the last time you spoke with her?"

"She was mad and yelling at me because I lost some money in a poker game. I'd been drinking. I pushed her down on the couch, and I left."

"Where did you go?"

"I rode my bike around just to cool off."

"Your bicycle?"

"No, I have a Harley in the garage."

"How long were you gone?" Kat asked.

"I don't know—an hour, maybe more. She was gone when I got back."

"What kind of vehicle does Judith drive?"

"She didn't. I think her sister came by and picked her up. They're just trying to get me in trouble for pushing her. I think she's over at her sisters. Have you been to her house yet?"

"What about the children?" Kat asked.

"They're both married and don't live here. Look, I have to get back to work. Can we get this over with?"

"Do you mind if I take a quick look around?"

"You have a warrant?"

"No. Do I need one?"

"Well, there's nothing here. Like I said, I really have to get back to work. If you don't have a warrant, I'll have to say no." Mr. Brown walked over, opened the front door, and made room for Kat to leave.

Kat sat in her car until Mr. Brown's car turned the corner. She then went and knocked on the neighbor's door.

Mrs. Pitts looked at her through the screen and told Kat about the cussing and verbal abuse exhibited by both parties over the past few years.

"Do you recall hearing a motorcycle around midnight last Saturday night?"

"I didn't hear anything that night, but that damn wood chipper was so loud my husband and I couldn't enjoy the game. That was all day Saturday."

"So you didn't hear a motorcycle or anything else?"

"No, I didn't, but my husband mentioned Sunday morning over breakfast that he saw Mr. Brown with a wood chipper behind his truck at two o'clock in the morning."

"Was he sure it was two o'clock?"

"Quite sure," said Mrs. Pitts. "He's seventy-two years old. I call him Dr. Pepper because he has to pee at ten, two, and four."

"Is your husband here now?" Kat asked. "I'd like to speak with him."

"No, he went to Home Depot to pick up some washers for a leaky faucet."

"So he will be back soon?"

"Not likely. He gets to wandering around that store and gets distracted. It may take him hours."

"Does he have a cell phone?" Kat asked. "Can I call him?"

"Ha, cell phone; that's funny. We still have an antenna for our TV."

Kat took a business card from her pocket and handed it to Mrs. Pitts, pointing to the phone number on it. "Please have him call me when he does return home." Kat thanked Mrs. Pitts but had no luck finding any of the other neighbors home that time of day.

57

The call she had been waiting for all morning finally came.

"Hey, kitten, looks like our assessment at the scene was spot on," said Ric. "The ME says we have two different calibers of weapons. The victims were facing forward in the vehicle. The shooter or shooters were behind them. Huerta had a .32 slug lodged against the inside of his skull. We sent it over to Ballistics already. Timms was shot with a larger caliber weapon; that's why the bullet exited his head and went out the top of the cruiser. Good luck finding that one."

"Is Javier still there?" she asked.

"No, he left. He was none too happy with the findings."

"Yeah, he kind of jumped the gun on his initial explanation of what took place."

"Are you thinking what I'm thinking?" Ric asked.

"Yes, but I'm not going to say out loud—not yet anyway." Kat thanked Ric and said, "I've got another call to make."

Joel picked up on the second ring.

Kat asked, "Did you find anything in the cruiser in the back seat?"

"We dusted for prints," Joel told her. "We also used small particle reagent to see if we could find any contents because the car was in the water. We found several prints, but they all appear to belong to Detective Aguilar—which makes sense because he pulled the car from the water. We're about to take it to the underground garage and spray it with luminal."

"Mind if I tag along?"

"Glove up, and be my guest."

58

Kat met Joel and Brenda in the underground parking garage. They'd used that site before when they needed total darkness to photograph the illumination of the luminol as it reacted to blood. Joel explained to Kat that luminol was used to detect minute traces of blood, even blood that had been covered by water, as if someone was trying to cover up a crime.

Kat smiled and nodded as though she had just learned a valuable lesson, even though she had known this for quite some time.

"Okay, let's do this." Joel sprayed the entire interior of the vehicle. Before he could finish spraying, an eerie green glow appeared on the window, dash, and headliner of the cruiser.

Brenda had already prepared her camera inside the vehicle to capture the image. She took several pictures as Joel sprayed the inside a second time. Joel looked at Kat and said, "The glow fades but will come back time and time again, each time we spray."

Another impressive fact that I already knew, Kat thought, but she just smiled and asked, "What do you see?"

"A lot of blood," said Brenda. "A *whole* lot of blood."

"Can you determine the directions the shots were fired from?" Kat asked.

"We both had training in blood spatter investigation," Joel said, "but you'd need to be an expert to render an opinion on this."

"Great," she muttered. "Just great." Raising her voice, she asked, "Did you find anything else?"

"Nothing at the scene," said Brenda. "We are about to go over it with the ALS."

"Pulling out all the stops," Joel chimed in.

It was so quiet in the garage that the sound of Kat's phone startled all three of them. She looked down at the screen and recognized the number as belonging to Chief Gibson.

"Afternoon, Chief," she said as the other two continued with their work.

"Where are you?" Chief asked. After Kat informed him, he said, "Get up to my office right away."

Guess I won't be seeing Ms. Olivarez today, Kat thought, and she dialed the number to reschedule.

59

Juanita ushered Kat straight into Chief Gibson's office. The chief was sitting behind his desk, and Detective Javier Aguilar was standing at the window, looking out over the bay. The chief had the only view of the outside world in the whole building.

She could tell that Javier was pretty worked up. Chief Gibson asked both of them to be seated. He began by saying, "The media is going to have a shit storm with this. First, we have a captain on leave, suspected of killing his own wife. Now this—two police officers shooting each other at close range."

"Excuse me, Chief ... you're saying that Huerta and Timms shot each other?" Kat asked.

"Yes, that's what was explained to me by Detective Aguilar."

"Did you get the reports from the ME's office?" Kat asked.

Javier jumped out of his chair. "What do you know about the autopsies? I was there! Dr. Elizondo said the origin of the bullets could not be determined. He said it looked like the officers were facing forward, but that's as far as he could go."

"So what does that mean to you?" Kat asked, looking straight at Javier.

"I think they got into an argument, and one or both pulled their guns, and shit happened."

"'Shit happened,' yeah. That'll look real good on a police report," Kat said as she rose to meet Javier's glare.

"Sit down," said the chief. "We've got to all be on the same page, especially you two. We have two hotshots coming in over the next few weeks. Javier, you are the acting captain. Detective Gonzales, we have spoken already about your duties. Not a word to the media. Hell, don't even talk to the other officers about this. That goes for both of you. Understood? Now get the hell out of my office!"

Kat and Javier exited the chief's office without a word to each other. Javier took the elevator, and Kat chose the stairs.

The next morning Kat suppressed her anger when she saw Javier sitting at Captain Moore's desk. "Motherfucker," she said under her breath. She checked her messages and listened to Mr. Pitts informing her that he would be available all day if she needed more information concerning the Browns. A six-foot-seven refrigerator-size man with reddish-blond hair entered the office. He stood patiently while Kat replaced the receiver in her phone's cradle.

"I'm Terrance Jones from Houston. I was instructed to report to Detective Aguilar. Is that you?"

"Not on your life." She pointed toward Captain Moore's office.

"Thank you kindly," said Jones as headed toward the glassed-in office.

Kat watched the exchange of introductions and grinned at how Jones towered over Javier. Moments later, she sensed the presence of someone else standing in the doorway. She saw a six-foot, slim-built man of about thirty-five, wearing a white shirt, gray slacks, and gray and red tie, with a hint of red in his socks. *Mr. GQ*, she thought.

He spoke. "I'm Jay Dee Baker, here from Austin to see—"

"Detective Aguilar. I know." She pointed at the other two men.

"And you are?" asked Jay Dee

"I'm Detective Katarina Gonzales."

"Looking forward to working with you, Detective Gonzales," he said as he shook Kat's hand. Then, excusing himself, he walked toward Captain Moore's office.

Kat remained seated and watched the interaction between the three men. *This is all I need*, she thought. *Three dicks and me.*

As she continued to watch through the glass, she returned Mr. Pitts's phone call. She asked him if he could recall what had occurred at the Browns' residence last Saturday.

"Yes, yes, Officer. They cut down some small trees in the backyard. They were using a wood chipper all afternoon. My wife and I were watching the game. We had the TV up as loud as it could go, but we still couldn't hear. I didn't say anything because he's not a very nice person."

"Can you tell me what you saw later on that night?"

"Yes, ma'am. I got up to go to the restroom, and I heard some commotion outside. I looked through the blinds in the front room, and I saw Mr. Brown pulling a wood chipper behind his truck."

"Are you sure it was Mr. Brown?" Kat asked.

"It was too dark. I couldn't see inside, but I know it was his truck."

"What time was that?" Kat asked.

"It was 2:05 a.m., exactly," Mr. Pitts replied. "I thought, What the hell is he doing at 2:05 with a wood chipper?"

"Did you see him return?" Kat asked.

"No, but when I got up at four o'clock, I looked out, and the truck and wood chipper were still gone. When I got up at six, they were both back in the driveway."

"When was the last time you saw Mrs. Brown?"

"I didn't see her, but I heard her yelling at him on Saturday afternoon, telling him to shut that damn thing off. He yelled at her to shut the F-word up. Then he started up again."

"Okay, thank you," said Kat. "If you think of anything else, please don't hesitate to call."

About that time, the door to Captain Moore's office opened, and out came Jones and Baker.

Kat went over to Huerta's desk, laid out some folders, and pushed them toward Jones. "These are yours," she said.

Walking across the room she laid some other folders on Timms's desk and pointed at Baker. "These are for you."

Then, against her normal routine of working alone, she asked Baker to come with her to canvas the neighbors of the missing person, Mrs. Brown.

Divide and conquer, Kat thought. *I'm not going to let these three team up against me. The good ole boys are gone.*

Jones sat down and began familiarizing himself with the cases in front of him, as Baker and Kat left the building.

"Tell me about yourself," Kat said, once they were in her Mustang.

"What do you want to know?" Baker replied.

"Your career, where'd you go to school, where'd you work?"

"I got my criminal justice degree from Sam Houston University. I started as a police officer of my hometown of Floresville, Texas. I took classes and went to as many seminars as I could, worked my way up, and got a job with the Texas Rangers. I've been working in Austin ever since."

"Solved any big cases?" Kat asked.

"A few," Baker replied. "Now what's this case we're working here?"

"We've got a Mrs. Brown who's been missing for about five days, according to her sister."

"Married?" Baker asked.

"Me or Mrs. Brown?" Kat laughed

"Both," said Baker.

"I'm single, but Mrs. Brown is married. Husband seemed like a jerk."

"But anybody might be a jerk if they hadn't been laid in five days," said Baker.

"Oh," said Kat, "so you're one of those?"

"I don't know what you mean by 'one of those,' but no, I'm not one of those," he said in a voice that mimicked Kat.

Kind of cocky, Kat thought, *but I like that.* Hell, she was cocky, and everyone knew it, even her.

She had a good feeling about Baker, even though it was way too early to be certain. Kat figured Baker would be easy to work with; he was certainly easy on the eyes. *Handsome devil,* she thought.

61

Kat parked across the street from the Browns' house. She noticed Mr. Brown's truck was not in the driveway.

"What did you say your first name was?" Kat asked.

"Jay Dee," he replied.

"What's the JD stand for?"

"No, it's not my initials. It's J-A-Y D-E-E. Don't ask me why. My parents have a funny sense of humor."

"And you? You have a funny sense of humor?"

"Not quite like theirs, but yes, I would say that I do."

"Well, okay, then, funny man Jay Dee. You take those two houses while I go to these." Kat pointed in the respective directions. "Try to find out if anyone has seen or heard from Mrs. Brown since Saturday. Also ask if they know anything about a wood chipper."

62

When Kat and Jay Dee returned to the car after fifteen minutes, Jay Dee said, "Nobody answered the door there"—he pointed across the street from the Pitts' residence—"but a Ms. Eckerdt next door said they were in San Antonio all weekend. They got home around seven on Sunday evening. She did say that the Browns were often yelling at each other, even in the front yard. Said she never saw physical violence, just cussing and screaming."

"Not much to go on. I didn't even get an answer. Either everyone here works during the day, or they are afraid to come to the door. Okay, let's go." Kat slid behind the wheel.

"Detective Gonzales, what's with the wood chipper?" Jay Dee asked.

"Kat. Call me Kat; everyone else does. The Pitts"—Kat pointed next door—"said the Browns used a wood chipper Saturday afternoon. Mr. Pitts said he saw Mr. Brown's truck pull away at two o'clock Sunday morning with the wood chipper in tow. Nobody has seen Mrs. Brown since then."

"Guess we need to locate that wood chipper," said Jay Dee.

"Not we, *you*," said Kat. "I'm headed over to the sister's house. She's the one who reported Mrs. Brown as missing."

"Done and done," said Jay Dee.

Kat quickly glanced at Jay Dee. "Okay, then."

Kat dropped off Jay Dee at the police station.

"Hey, how about you ask the other guy—Jones, is it?—to come along with me on this while you track down the chipper."

"The other guy—yeah, I'll tell him," said Jay Dee as he walked toward the building.

"Let's get the low-down on Jones," Kat mumbled as she dialed Roxanne's number.

Roxanne picked up right away. "Hey there, kitten, you okay? Damn, doesn't pay to be a detective for Corpus PD. What's going on over there?"

"Don't have long to talk. I'll fill you in tonight. We have two temps filling in. One is as big as a house; he's from Houston. The other one is from—"

"Is he a midget?" Roxanne interrupted. "You didn't mention his size. I thought you might be trying to be politically correct."

"It's 'little people' and no, he's not a little person. He's good size," said Kat.

"Good size," said Roxanne. "What exactly do you mean by that? You follow him into the men's room or what?"

"Get your mind out of the gutter. Hey, gotta go. Man mountain is almost here. See you tonight." Kat rang off.

Terrance Jones deftly managed to get his six-foot-seven, 265-pound frame into the front seat of the Mustang.

"You can push the seat back if you like," Kat said once Jones closed his passenger-side door.

"Believe I might. Thank you kindly," said Jones.

"I'm Kat," she said, extending her hand.

Jones fingers extended about three inches past Kat's wrist as he shook her hand. "Terrance Jones, but call me T. Pleased to be working with you, Kat," he drawled.

"You aren't from Texas, are you?" she asked.

"No, ma'am, I was born in Arkansas."

"What brings you to Texas?"

"Football. I received a scholarship to play ball at Sam Houston."

"I knew it. I watched the interaction through the window in Captain Moore's office. You two didn't let on that you knew each other, but I could tell something was up. Javier doesn't have a clue does he?"

"If you are referring to Captain Aguilar, then no ma'am. Neither of us mentioned that we were friends."

"Captain Aguilar!" Kat screamed, almost coming out of her seat. "He's *not* captain. He's just filling in while Captain Moore is on leave. Aguilar is a detective, just like me. Javier is already calling himself *captain*? We'll see about that."

"Sorry, Detective, I didn't know. Just got a call yesterday to be in Corpus Christi, ready to roll today at 8:00 a.m. sharp."

"No, no, it's I who should apologize." Kat gave T the short version of what had happened over the last few days. "Thank you and Baker for helping out."

"Sounds like the making of a good movie or TV series, if you ask me," said T.

"Let's hope not," said Kat. "Why 'T'?"

"I've been called T since I was a kid. I use Terrance Jones in my profession and save T for my friends. Please, you call me T. I look forward to working with you, Kat. Where to now?"

"Headed to see the sister of a missing person. Her name is Barbara Olivarez; the missing sister is Judith Brown. Last seen by neighbors Saturday afternoon."

"You suspect foul play?" T asked.

"We do have a movie plot. There may be a wood chipper involved. I've got Baker running down that lead."

"You never know what the day holds, do you?" T chuckled.

"And it's not even noon," Kat said. "How long have you two known each other? Did you meet at Sam Houston?"

"We've been best friends since kindergarten. My dad was an Arkansas state trooper. He moved us to a little town thirty minutes south of Little

Rock, where he worked, a town called Redfield on the Arkansas River. Great place to grow up."

"You said he 'was' a trooper. Is your dad retired?"

"No, ma'am. He was shot and killed in the line of duty when I was in sixth grade."

"I'm terribly sorry," said Kat.

"Thank you; it's okay. It was hard at the time. Single mother raising four older sisters and me. She used to say I ate more groceries than the other five of them put together." T smiled.

"I can imagine. I have four older brothers myself." Kat felt herself opening up to this stranger who didn't feel like a stranger at all. T had a presence that exuded security.

"I almost failed sixth grade, but Jay Dee's dad was a coach and teacher at the junior high. He worked with me after school and got me caught up. He also kinda took over as a second dad. Always took me hunting and fishing with him and Jay Dee. He was a great coach too."

"I hate to ask, but you said 'was' again. Is he gone too?" Kat asked.

"Oh no, still coaching high school football. Our senior year he took a job in Floresville. Mrs. Baker—she's Hispanic—grew up there. Her mother became ill after her dad passed, so they moved back to Texas to look after Jay Dee's grandma. She wasn't about to move to Arkansas, so I lost my best buddy. It was hard on everybody."

"I know how stubborn old Hispanic women can be—men too," said Kat. "Thankfully, both my parents are still alive. They can get on my nerves, especially my mom, who's always trying to fix me up, but I love 'em both to death."

"So you aren't married," T said with a grin.

"And you are?" Kat asked.

"Yep, married my college sweetheart twelve years ago. She was a cheerleader, and I was in love the first time I laid eyes on her. I get the shimmies just thinking about her. Can't believe she's with a big ole ox like me."

"Shimmies." Kat laughed. "Do you take medication for that? Never heard of the shimmies."

"You know, your body starts to wiggle in place, and you get that happy feeling like a kid eating a snow cone," T explained.

"No shimmies for me," Kat said. "Must not have met the right person."

"Guess not," T replied.

64

Kat pulled her Mustang into the drive of the Olivarez residence. She knocked on the door, turned to T, and said, "I didn't call ahead. I wanted to arrive unannounced, if you get my drift."

"Got it."

Barbara Olivarez answered the door, looking surprised. She was wearing a T-shirt without a bra, shorts, and flip-flops. "Hang on one minute," she said as she closed the door, returning moments later wearing a pullover sweater. "Please come in. Forgive me. I wasn't expecting company."

Kat and T took a seat on the sofa facing the TV. *The Price Is Right* was still on as Mr. Olivarez clicked the remote to off.

Kat was about to ask a question when T spoke first.

"Please excuse me, ma'am. I had a ton of coffee on the way over here. Can I use your restroom? Won't take but a minute."

Reluctantly, Mrs. Olivarez pointed down the hall. "Second door on your left."

T ambled toward the restroom as Kat began her questioning.

T walked past the restroom and began opening doors on both sides of the hallway. The first bedroom was empty, except for kids' toys strewn about the floor. When he opened the second door, he saw a middle-aged woman sitting in the middle of the bed, holding a glass of what appeared to be iced tea. "Mrs. Brown?" said T.

"Yes."

"You wanna come with me into the living room," T said.

Without a word, Judith Brown walked in front of T toward the voices coming from the living room. Mrs. Olivarez stopped midsentence as her sister entered the room.

Kat recognized Judith Brown immediately from the photographs in her case folder. "Mrs. Brown, are you okay?" Kat asked.

"No, no, I'm not okay," Judith Brown said. "My husband is trying to kill me. He said he was going to chop me up into little pieces and throw me into that damn wood chipper. He's crazy enough to do it too. I had to get away."

"So you've been here all along?" Kat asked as she looked at Barbara Olivarez.

Mrs. Olivarez spoke up. "We figured Pete would think she was hiding, so I called her in as missing to throw him off."

"So you have been hiding from your husband, Pete. Are you ready to file a complaint against him for threatening your life?" Kat asked, even though she knew the answer.

"No, he'll cool off; he always does. He's just been in a tough spot these last few weeks. I was just getting ready to go back home anyway," Judith said.

"That's not a good idea," Kat told her. "I talked with your husband. He seemed quite agitated. The only way we can secure your safety is if you file a formal complaint against Pete. We can take him into custody and not release him until he calms down."

"I'm not gonna file," Judith said.

Kat looked sternly at Barbara Olivarez. "It's against the law to file a false missing persons claim."

Judith quickly said, "We're sorry; we didn't mean to break the law. We just needed a diversion so Pete wouldn't come here. I'm so sorry. It won't happen again."

"Fine." Kat threw up her hands in disgust, turned to T, and asked, "You ready?"

Once back in her Mustang, Kat said, "You didn't have a drop of coffee coming over here. How the hell did you know she was in the house?"

"I didn't know for sure it was Mrs. Brown, but somebody was there," T said. "I saw a damp circle on the coffee table when we sat down. Mrs. Olivarez was drinking coffee; her cup wouldn't leave a ring like that. Somebody had to have had a cold glass of something for that condensation to form and run down the glass."

"I'll be damned, Sherlock. Solved the first case in minutes."

T grinned. "Sometimes you get chicken; sometimes you get feathers."

65

When they returned to the office, Jay Dee was just hanging up the phone. "I found it," he said.

"Found what?" T asked.

"The wood chipper Mr. Brown rented. It's still on the lot. Hasn't been used since he returned it. I was headed there to check it out. Got any Hemident handy?" Jay Dee asked.

"Yes, we have Hemident, but you don't need it. Mrs. Brown's still intact. Ace, here, found her hiding out at her sister's."

"Damn good police work, Jones," said Jay Dee.

"Cut the crap, Baker," said Kat. "I got the life stories of the both of you, thanks to Ace, here."

"T. My name is T, not Ace."

"Roger that," said Kat. She turned to Jay Dee. "He always this corny?"

"You have no idea," Jay Dee said.

"Well, in that case, I'm going over to the DA's office. Got an incident—guy at a strip club sneaks his own bottle into the place, gets snockered, goes out the back door, tries to cross six lanes of traffic, and doesn't make it past lane four. Other than a faulty alarm on the emergency exit, I don't see the club being held responsible, but that's up to powers higher than me. Should be enough on your desks to keep you and *T* busy until I see you again—tomorrow."

"Roger that," said T.

Kat grinned. "Don't call me Roger."

66

Rather than going downtown to the DA's office, Kat called and reported her findings over the phone. Her Mustang was already headed toward Roxanne's. "Beer, wine, or whiskey?" Kat asked when Roxanne answered the call.

"Tough choice," said Roxanne. "I like all three. How about a three-legged monkey?"

"A what monkey?" Kat asked.

"It's a drink I get at Dr. Rockets—Crown, amaretto, pineapple juice, and grenadine to sweeten it. Fuckin' awesome; you'll love it."

"Sounds fine to me. Be there in twenty," said Kat.

Roxanne had two double shots waiting as Kat came up the steps. She handed Kat her drink. "Bottoms up, babe."

Both women took a long drink, Roxanne almost killing hers.

Kat was more cautious. "Damn, this is good," she said as she downed the rest. "Keep 'em coming, love."

"So," said Roxanne. "Tell me about the new boys."

"Both about our age. The one from Houston is six foot seven, married, a country boy from Arkansas. The other is from Austin. His name is Jay Dee—that's J-A-Y D-E-E."

"And?" Roxanne coaxed. "Single?"

"He's a little under six foot, sharp dresser, seems nice."

"Okay, okay, he has a great personality, mends his own socks, and is a great cook. Ugly, huh?"

Kat looked sheepishly up at Roxanne. "I got wet when I saw him, girl."

"Good-looking, snazzy dresser, single—my gaydar is going off the charts."

Kat shook her head. "I didn't get that feeling. He probably has a girlfriend, though. What are the odds?"

"Any guy that wets your panties definitely has a girlfriend, probably more than one."

"Enough," said Kat. "There's something wrong with my glass."

"What's that?" asked Roxanne.

Kat laughed. "It's empty."

When Kat arrived at the office the following morning, she saw empty chairs, and Javier was drinking coffee behind Captain Moore's desk.

"Where's Mutt and Jeff?" She pointed toward the empty office. "They on banker's hours?"

"Jones is working one of Timms's cases; Baker has one of Huerta's, or vice versa. I'm not sure."

"Good to know," Kat said. After a pause, she said, "Detective …" She turned toward her desk and said over her shoulder, "And you? What do you have working?"

Standing up, he said angrily, "You know damn well what I have working. Two of our friends are dead."

"*Your* friends," Kat corrected him and left it at that.

Later that afternoon she decided to spice things up. Jay Dee and T were both back in the office putting the final touches on a day's work.

"What do you make of this?" Kat asked as she laid out the folder containing photographs from inside the vehicle in which Huerta and Timms were killed. Kat explained the scenario that prompted both of them to be pulled from their regular duties to help out in Corpus Christi.

"Detective Aguilar sees this as the men having shot each other because each wanted the captain's job," Kat said.

After a few minutes, T said, "Shooter or shooters were in the back seat."

"No doubt," Jay Dee agreed.

"Do you have the expertise to testify to that fact?" Kat asked.

"No, but I know someone who does," T replied as he looked at Jay Dee.

"Nash," Jay Dee and T said simultaneously.

"Who?" asked Kat.

"Dr. Graham Nash," Jay Dee said. "He was one of our instructors at Sam Houston."

"Knows this stuff inside and out," said T. "Best I have ever seen at blood spatter."

"Well, let's email him these photos and see what your Dr. Nash has to say," said Kat.

"It's Friday night. He won't get these until Monday, maybe Tuesday," said Jay Dee.

"Call and let him know," said Kat.

Both men chuckled. "No cell phone," said T. "Doesn't want to be bothered. He's probably making love to a bottle of Jack Daniel's by now."

"This guy is really that good?" Kat asked.

"He's that good," said Jay Dee.

"Glad you fellas didn't have plans for Saturday," said Kat. "Looks like we will be paying your expert an unexpected visit tomorrow—that is, if you think you two can locate where he'll be."

T and Jay Dee glanced at each other. T raised his eyebrows while Jay Dee raised his shoulder and turned over his left hand, signaling to Kat that they could indeed locate Dr. Graham Nash.

"I know a great taco stand in Portland. Eat on the way," Kat said.

"We're not taking your car, I hope," T said.

Kat laughed. "We'll take a cruiser, but I will drive. Meet you two here at seven tomorrow morning."

68

Kat picked up the keys to a Ford LTD, the vehicle of choice by the upper echelon in the Corpus PD. She noticed T sitting behind the wheel of a Toyota Tundra; Jay Dee was in the passenger side. A Toyota Solara convertible was parked nearby.

"Figures," Kat said aloud as she passed the sports car. Jay Dee walked behind the LTD and slid into the front passenger seat; T climbed in the back. *Alpha*, Kat thought.

"Good morning, Kat," T said, smiling into her rearview mirror.

"Yes, good morning, Kat," chimed in Jay Dee. "Look, if you want to take turns driving, we'll be happy to switch. It's a long drive."

"Thanks," said Kat. "Have you been waiting long?"

"Not at all," replied T.

"Tacos?" Kat asked as she pulled out of the parking lot and onto Ocean Drive.

"Sure is pretty here," Jay Dee said.

"Yes, it is," said Kat.

"Have you been here long?" T asked.

"Born and raised in Alice," Kat began.

"Alice, Alice, who the fuck is Alice?" yelled T. "Pardon my French, ma'am."

Kat turned toward Jay Dee as though expecting an explanation.

"From an old song by Dr. Hook," Jay Dee said. "Don't pay him any mind; he can't help himself."

After crossing the harbor bridge connecting Corpus Christi with the small town of Portland, Kat took the first exit and pulled into an old hamburger drive-through that was now operating as a taco stand. "Bacon, egg, and avocado with a Dr. Pepper," came the breakfast order from the back seat.

Kat leaned back for Jay Dee to speak into the drive-through microphone. "Bean, egg, and avocado, with a small coffee, please."

Kat turned and ordered, "Potato, egg, and add some avocado."

"Anything to drink with the last order?" asked the voice from the speaker.

"No," said Kat. *I'm not about to be the first to ask for a potty break.*

With their order collected, Kat pulled out onto the highway again.

"Good taco," Jay Dee said.

A muffled "Um-hm" came from the back as T stuffed another bite into his mouth.

"Not a coffee drinker?" Kat asked T.

"Not when it's this hot; no, ma'am. I get my caffeine right here." He held up his bottle of Dr. Pepper.

"So you're lifelong friends, right?" Kat said. "Jay Dee, T said you two met in kindergarten."

T leaned forward, finished with his taco. "Well, we were five years old. I was riding my bicycle around the new neighborhood when I saw some underwear and a shirt laying there on the road. I could hear singing coming from an uncovered manhole. I got off my bike and looked over the edge. That's the first time I laid eyes on this guy."

"You fell in?" Kat asked Jay Dee.

"I wanted to see how deep the hole was," Jay Dee said. "I slipped and got a firsthand view."

"Singing?" asked Kat.

"I was down there a long time. Seemed like hours to me, but it probably wasn't thirty minutes. I tossed my shirt and underwear up out of the hole, hoping somebody would see. I kept my shorts in case I got rescued. It was too hard to climb out—believe me, I tried."

"Ten feet or so to the bottom," T said. "I know that because I got my older sisters. They brought a twelve-foot ladder and there wasn't much sticking up above the hole."

Kat glanced at Jay Dee. "Damn! Were you injured?"

T answered, "Naw, we put the ladder down there, and he climbed right out. He said thanks, put on his shirt, turned to me, and said, 'Hi, I'm Jay Dee. Who are you?'"

"What did your parents say?"

Jay Dee said, "Didn't tell them. I didn't want my old man to know I was stupid enough to fall into a hole in the middle of the road."

"That was a dangerous situation," said Kat.

"It was roped off and had warning signs—everything a five-year-old boy needs to draw his attention. I was fortunate that I didn't get hurt."

"Fortunate indeed," agreed Kat.

T said, "Yep, we got off to an exciting start, and it's never been boring since. Tell her about the bottle rockets at the arsenal."

"Yes," said Kat, "tell her about all that."

Jay Dee grinned. "Around New Year's we would all pitch in and buy as many fireworks as we could. Somebody got the bright idea to shoot 'em off on the 'vidock' going to the arsenal."

"Near our hometown there's a huge area, thousands of acres," T interjected. "The army conducted experiments there, secret stuff, nobody knows what. Anyway, there's an overpass for trains to cross under a short distance from the main gate. We called it the *vidock*."

"Oh, and you boys shot bottle rockets off the vidock, as you called it?"

"No, we fired off a twister," said T. "It went about thirty feet into the air and lit up the whole viaduct like it was noon."

"It was bright," Jay Dee agreed. "We shot off a couple of firecrackers, got scared, and ran to the car parked down the other side of the viaduct from the guardhouse."

"As we were running down the hill," T said, "two fellows come walking from the tracks below, and one says, 'Hey, Jay Dee.'"

"They recognized you? Who were they?" asked Kat.

"Don't know," said Jay Dee. "I said 'Hey' and kept running. To this day I don't know who they were or even what they were doing in the middle of nowhere, with not another vehicle in sight."

"They didn't report you? You didn't get into trouble?"

"No, my girlfriend at the time was the daughter of the commander at the arsenal. She told me the next day that they'd had a red-alert drill, that somebody fired shots at the guardhouse."

"They say if you fire a shot into the arsenal," T said, "that they will chase you until you stop running or they catch you."

Kat laughed. "Is there a reward out for you fellas?"

"Not for that," T said.

"Where do the bottle rocks fit in?" ask Kat.

"Later that same evening, we were shooting bottle rockets out of my mom's car," said Jay Dee.

"We just shot at the people we knew," said T, as if that made a difference.

"How do you *shoot* bottle rockets out of a moving vehicle?" Kat asked.

"My mom had just bought a Buick LeSabre from my grandmother," Jay Dee explained. "We got hand-me-down vehicles. My dad was a coach, and my mom stayed home to raise my two sisters and younger brother and me. Tough times. I can't believe she let me drive the Buick."

"You're the oldest?" asked Kat.

"Yes. Anyway, we had four guys in the back of that monster, and T was sitting up front with me."

"We had it down," T told her. "The guy sitting behind me would roll down the back window; the guy next to him would hold a hollow tent pole that he could aim it at cars, houses, whatever. He was pretty good at it. The third guy had a thick mitten on his hand."

"A mitten? What the hell?" Kat said, shaking her head.

"Yeah, the fourth guy would light the bottle rocket—one of those quarter-miler rockets. Then the guy with the mitten would shove it into the tent pole and keep his hand over the back opening, so the rocket would go out the front. The mitten protected his hand."

Kat laughed. "With such precision, how could anything go wrong?"

"Well, it did," said Jay Dee. "Seems the mitten guy didn't get the rocket loaded, and it came out the back of the pole and flew around the back of the Buick."

"Oh my! What did you do?"

"We ducked," Jay Dee and T said in unison.

"Jay Dee, you were driving at this time?"

"Yes," answered Jay Dee.

T said, "The fellas in the back were screaming. Sparks and smoke were everywhere, and this guy"—he tapped Jay Dee's shoulder—"was yelling, 'Don't let it get on the upholstery!'"

"The car was new to us," said Jay Dee. "I didn't want to ruin my mom's car. Luckily, the rocket didn't pop. We would be wearing hearing aids if it had."

"Your mom's car was okay?"

"Yes, we opened all the windows, turned the vents up high, and let it air out. We never did that again."

"Bet the police in your town just loved you two." Kat smiled.

"George had it in for us, especially Jay Dee."

"Must I ask who George was?"

Jay Dee nodded. "Small town. We had two police officers. Benny, the older guy, had the day shift, and George was out nights. He stopped me almost every weekend."

"That could be construed as harassment," said Kat, almost sounding alarmed.

"I'll never forget one night when T and I had two girls in my dad's Volkswagen Beetle," Jay Dee said.

"Kim and Sharon," T remembered.

"Yes," Jay Dee said. "We had been drinking."

"How old were you?" asked Kat.

"Probably eighteen," said T.

"So were you of legal drinking age then?"

"Nope. Arkansas has always been twenty-one, not eighteen like Texas was for a while," said Jay Dee.

"Well, how did you get alcohol?"

"Jay Dee's been buying since he was sixteen. Hell, the boy had a mustache in junior high."

"Peach fuzz," Jay Dee said. "Anyway, there was nothing going on, and nobody had any ideas, so I would drive my dad's bug up the hill, push in the clutch, and roll backward down the hill, asking each time, 'What ya want to do?' After about the fourth time, I saw George coming up in the rearview mirror. When he hit the blue lights, I thought we were done for. George was finally going to get his bust."

"What did you do?" Kat asked.

"I asked T for some gum. He gave me some Juicy Fruit still in the foil wrapper. I started chewing it before I realized that. Do you know how bad that metallic taste is?"

"Can't say that I've ever experienced that, no, but I bet it wasn't pleasant," Kat said.

"It's not," said Jay Dee. "So I got the foil off the gum, and by this time, George was at my window. He stuck his head inside, smelling for weed or alcohol, no doubt."

"No doubt," Kat agreed.

"He says, 'I've been sitting over there at the bank, watching you go up and down this hill. What y'all been drinking? Vodka?'"

"What had you been drinking?" Kat asked.

"Beer," said T. "Lots of beer. All four of us were toasted."

"I knew when George said vodka that he couldn't smell anything, so I felt our chances were pretty good of getting away with it. I said, 'Nothing. We've not been drinking.'"

"Bet that pissed him off," said Kat.

"Actually, he acted real friendly. He said, 'I'm not going to do anything. I just want to know what y'all had to drink tonight.' I pointed at T and said he had a Dr. Pepper, the girls had cherry Cokes, and I had a Sprite."

"What happened?" Kat asked.

"He left," said T. "I thought Kim was going to pee her pants when Jay Dee was talking to George, but he just left."

The next few hours disappeared as Kat, Jay Dee, and T took turns telling stories from their childhood, one hell-raising event topped by another.

Kat felt safe in the company of these two men. She wasn't in competition, and she didn't need to put on airs. They were just country boys with no hidden agenda. They were there to just get the job done; she appreciated that.

69

Following Jay Dee's directions, Kat navigated her way through Huntsville. About a mile outside the city limits, she pulled into the drive of a white two-story colonial with a huge front porch. The roof needed work, but other than that, Kat was impressed with the façade. It even had a porch swing. "Love it," Kat said.

"Yeah, pretty cool, huh?" T agreed.

Jay Dee wasted little time crossing the immaculate lawn and petting two Labrador retrievers as they rose from the porch to greet the visitors.

A thin man appeared, opening the screen door. Kat assumed this was Dr. Nash. He was about five foot nine and in his midsixties. What hair he had left was starting to gray a bit. *Let's see what this man can do*, she thought, hoping the six-hour drive wasn't for naught.

"I swear I didn't do it," Dr. Nash said, laughing. "Do you boys have a warrant?" He noticed Kat looking for a sidewalk so she wouldn't disturb the nice lawn. "My, my. What have we here?" Not waiting for an introduction, Dr. Nash met Kat at the top of the steps. "I'm Dr. Graham Nash. You can call me Graham. These two accomplices of yours can call me Dr. Nash."

Kat shook Graham's hand and said, "I'm Katarina Gonzales, detective, Corpus Christi PD. Pleased to meet you, Dr. Nash."

"No, no, no, call me Graham. Please, have a seat. May I offer you something to drink? Sweet tea?"

"No, I'm fine. Thank you, though," said Kat.

"A restroom then?" Graham offered. "Right down the hall; it's the door under the stairs. Be my guest." Turning to the two men, he said, "You fellas can go pee off the back porch."

Kat took Graham up on his offer and felt much relief. As she came back out to the porch, she saw Dr. Nash positioned on the right side of the swing. He patted the left side gently. "Please sit down, Detective. Tell me what has brought you three up here so far from home."

Kat seated herself in the swing beside Graham and handed him the photos. "These are two of our detectives—or I should I say, *were*."

Dr. Nash took the folder and began slightly rocking the swing as he studied each photo. "What is it, exactly, that you want me to see?"

"The position of the shooter or shooters," Kat replied, not wanting to give too much information before he could reach his own conclusion.

"Obviously, the shooter or shooters were in the back seat. The spatter indicates that the gun or guns were held not far from the heads and at an angle that could only come from the back seat," said Dr. Nash.

"You are sure?" asked Kat, as Jay Dee and T reappeared from the side of the house.

"Oh, no doubt about it, my dear. Did you take these photos?"

"Our crime scene tech did."

"Well, he or she can work a scene with me anytime," said Graham. "Tell your tech he does good work, really good."

"I certainly will," Kat said, reaching for the folder.

Nash held on to one photo. "Look here. See the spatter on the headliner? Fantastic shot. Shooters got blood all over them as well, open and shut. Is your suspect in custody?"

T and Jay Dee sat in rocking chairs facing Kat and Dr. Nash.

"No," said Kat. "The lead investigator is calling this a case of two detectives shooting each other, possibly over an argument."

"Well, either he is an idiot, or he's trying to cover up something," said Dr. Nash. "Are these men gay?"

"Not likely," replied Kat.

"Who was first on the scene?" asked Graham.

"A Detective Aguilar," said Kat. "He's also the lead investigator."

"Did you work the scene?" he asked.

"I was there. I just don't buy Aguilar's explanation."

"Good girl," Nash said sincerely. "Was there blood on this Aguilar?"

"Not that I saw … but I did notice his shirt was crisp, not wrinkled."

"Time of day?" asked Graham.

"Three thirty in the morning," replied Kat.

"Hmm."

"What does *hmm* mean?" asked Kat.

"Hmm means hmm," replied Nash. "I cannot venture a guess. I go by the evidence, and this evidence tells me that the shooter or shooters were leaning forward in the back seat and that they should have had an ample amount of blood on their faces and clothing, unless they were wearing masks, but at least it would have been on their shirts."

"Thank you," Kat said.

"Any evidence found in the back seat?" asked Nash.

"None. Aguilar said he pulled the vehicle from the Gulf. Saltwater washed away any trace evidence."

"Somebody was clever. Hope you catch him." Standing, Graham said, "I'm sure you must be famished after driving all the way from Corpus. Let me fix you lunch."

"Your pork tenderloin sandwich?" T asked with high expectations.

"My boy, I see your tastes have not changed. Yes, I do believe I can grant such a request. It'll take a few minutes. Detective Gonzales, would you please accompany me to the kitchen and provide these two fine young men with some liquid refreshment?"

"My pleasure," said Kat as she left the comfort of the porch swing. "And please call me Kat."

"I most certainly will," said Graham as the two disappeared inside.

70

Kat returned to the porch carrying three glasses of ice-cold lemonade. Rising to take their glasses, the men thanked Kat. She took her spot on the swing.

"What do you think?" asked T. "What's your take on Dr. Nash?"

"I'd say listening to you boys reminisce about old times was well worth it. He is quite remarkable," said Kat.

"We've used him dozens of times in the Texas Rangers' office in Houston."

"FBI uses him too," said Jay Dee. "Hell, he was asked to go to LA for the OJ trial, but Dr. Henry Lee agreed first."

"Why does he stay here?" asked Kat. "He diddle the coeds?"

"Never," said Jay Dee.

"But he does their moms," T said with a laugh.

Jay Dee grinned and nodded.

"Real charmer," said T.

Kat pursed her lips. "Snake charmer," she said, but she was very impressed with his knowledge.

"Lunch on the veranda," came the call through the screen door.

Kat took her place between Jay Dee and T. The table was set with colorful Mikasa china that she had seen and liked in a catalog. A fresh-cut flower adorned a vase sitting slightly askew from the middle of the table. The linen napkins had a design that she couldn't quite make out, but it was coordinated with the china.

"This lemonade is very good," said Kat after taking a sip.

"Arnold Palmer," said Graham, "with a twist of lime, sweetened with fresh honey. Good for allergies."

Without hesitation, T and Jay Dee picked up their sandwiches and took healthy bites. Kat's first bite was a bit more cautious; her second bite was not. "This is fantastic," said Kat between chews.

"Seasoned pork tenderloin, topped with a medium fried egg, smoked Gouda, and fresh spinach on my killer wheat bread. The sweet cherry tomatoes and avocado on the side are topped with fresh-squeezed lemons. I'm glad you like it, Kat."

"Awesome," T said as he took another bite.

"Yes, very good. It brings back fond memories. Thank you, Dr. Nash!" Jay Dee said.

Dr. Nash looked at Kat and smiled. "My dear Kat, it seems you have fallen into the good fortune of sitting between the two best students I ever taught. And believe me—I have taught some good ones. Please tell me more about yourself and how it came to be that the best the Rangers has to offer are now in Corpus Christi."

Kat shared her story of making her way through the Corpus PD and reaching the rank of detective. She omitted the case of Captain Moore but felt comfortable talking about herself in front of the three men, who all listened intently.

When Kat finished talking, Graham rose and said, "Dessert."

All three declined.

"Nonsense! It's Diet Coke cake. I made it this morning. It should be cooled by now." He went back to the kitchen.

"I take it you fellas have eaten here before," said Kat.

"All the time," T said.

"Poor boys at college," Jay Dee said as Graham reentered the room, pushing a serving table as though he was a waiter in a five-star restaurant.

"You never served us dessert like that," said T.

Graham placed a large slice of chocolate cake covered with whip cream and fresh strawberries in front of Kat. "Picked the strawberries myself this morning," he said, beaming. "It's made with Diet Coke, my dear—no milk or eggs so please enjoy. Have you had this before?"

"No, first time," replied Kat.

"The carbonation of the soda causes the cake mix to rise," explained Graham.

"I think it's sweeter than regular cake," said Jay Dee. "I actually prefer it."

T took three bites and then pushed his mostly uneaten portion away.

"You don't care for it, Mr. Jones?" asked Graham. "You used to eat almost the entire cake by yourself. I often considered making two—one for you and another for everyone else. You can't let that piece go to waste. Eat up."

"I can't. It will go to my waist," said T. "Carolynn won't like me coming back from Corpus overweight."

"Don't tell me you married Carolynn Alexander," said Graham, seeming almost shocked.

"I don't get it either," said Jay Dee, "but yes, he did."

"She was, without a doubt, the most beautiful girl to have ever donned a cheerleading uniform and graced the sidelines for the Bearcats." Turning to face T, he teased, "How in the world did you manage to marry her?"

"Well, we were behind, late in the fourth quarter against Kingsville. The offense was on the field, so I was sitting on the bench, near the end. I looked over and saw Carolynn staring at me. She mouthed, 'Kick their ass,' clear as day. I could almost hear her say it. The offense fumbled, so I had to go on the field. I was so charged up I got past my man, and I intercepted a toss back to the running back. Then I hauled ass seventy-five yards for a touchdown. We won the game. Afterward, as we were walking off the field, she came and gave me a big kiss. I was in love from that moment on. Guess she was too, 'cause we started dating and got married right after college."

"I'll be damned," said Graham. "I recall that play now. Carolynn Alexander. I'll be."

Kat, now feeling a little like chopped liver, said, "This was very good, Graham. I so appreciate your taking the time to render an opinion on the case. And your hospitality was phenomenal—best lunch I've ever eaten."

71

Jay Dee drove on the way back to Corpus Christi. Kat sat in the front passenger seat, feeling much better about the trip now than before they'd started out. T sprawled out in the back seat, and a light snoring sound could be heard before they made it out of Huntsville.

"So this Caroline must be a looker, huh?" Kat said.

"Caro*lynn*," said Jay Dee. "Yes, she certainly is."

"What about you?" she asked. "You catch a pass, win a game, get the girl and all?"

"I've caught plenty of *passes*," Jay Dee said, glancing over at Kat.

"Ever married?" she asked.

"No. Close one time. I loved her, but she didn't love me. Or should I say she didn't love me enough. She wanted a career."

"What did she do?" asked Kat.

"Forensic psychologist. We met on a case in San Antonio. She was an instructor at the university. She wanted the big time. FBI came calling, and bam, she was off to Quantico. With Austin to San Antonio, we could make it work. Texas to Virginia—not happening." He kept his eyes on the road as he said, "So what do you do when the woman you love doesn't love you?"

"You move on," Kat said flatly.

"And when you can't move on?"

"You move over," replied Kat.

The two traveled in silence for at least an hour before Kat said, "Have you worked on any juicy cases?"

"Yes," said T, pulling himself up, using the back of the front seat for leverage.

"Well, let's hear about it," said Kat.

"After my injury," T said.

"How were you injured?" Kat asked.

"Car accident between junior and senior year of college. I got T-boned, messed up my knee and shoulder, and couldn't play senior season. Coaches wanted to get me another year of eligibility, but I said no. I wanted to graduate, get a job, and start a family. Sure, I'd wanted to play pro ball, but with an injury like mine, I didn't think it could happen."

"Any residual effects from the accident?" Kat asked.

"I can't play the piano," T replied.

"Why is that?" Kat asked. "Were you a good piano player before the accident?"

"He couldn't play before the accident either," said Jay Dee, stifling a laugh.

"Get serious," said Kat.

"Okay, this is serious; this really did happen," said T. "When I got out of the hospital after the accident, I found out the damn jerk who hit me didn't even have insurance. I needed money. I was in a bar when the manager said, 'You look like you could be a bouncer. You want a job?' I'd never been a bouncer before, but she said that wasn't a problem. She said I should show up at seven—"

"I thought we were talking about cases we worked on," Kat said, realizing T was starting another rambling story, "not another blast from the past."

"This is good," said Jay Dee. "Just wait; this is really good."

Kat sighed wearily but relented. "All right. Please continue."

T began again. "I got there the next day; it was a slow night. I was to just watch the floor and try to stop anything before it got out of hand. Not much was happening with only a few customers sitting at the bar. Then a couple in the back toward the pool table starts yelling. As I looked up, the man punched the woman in the face—square in the face. I came unglued. I was in Superman mode to save this damsel in distress. I ran across the room and punched this guy with all I had. I really let him have it.

"He went sailing over the side railing, over the pool table, and onto the floor. I ran around the pool table and was standing over this guy … when I noticed he didn't have any legs. I thought I'd knocked him in half."

"What happened to his legs?" Kat asked, wondering if she was being taken for a ride.

"They were still on the stool where he was sitting," said T.

"No way." Now she was sure this was a farce.

"Just wait," said Jay Dee.

"He had fake legs," T explained. "Prosthetic legs. He had unhooked them because they didn't sit right on the stool. So when I hit him, his upper torso just took off like a rocket. I felt like shit. I picked him up and carried him into the men's room, apologizing on the way—I was afraid he might sue me."

Kat asked, "What did he say?"

"He said that he wasn't going to sue. He said this was the first time since his surgery that anybody treated him like a real man. Everyone treated him different because he lost his legs. He actually thanked me."

"How did he lose his legs? I mean originally, not when you knocked them loose."

"Semitruck ran over his vehicle, trapped him inside, and smashed his legs. They had to be amputated. He said it messed him up bad; he couldn't have sex. That was his wife that he'd hit. She had just told him that she was having an affair and that she was leaving his sorry ass. He said he got so mad he just hauled off and punched her. I felt bad for the guy."

"Did you get fired?" asked Kat.

"No, I quit. I wasn't cut out for that kind of work."

"That didn't happen," said Kat suspiciously.

"Oh, it happened all right," said Jay Dee. "Every time we went to that bar, people got out of our way, even the bouncers. I'll bet they still talk about the guy who launched a patron across the room."

"I have to admit that's a good story," said Kat. "Thanks for sharing, but how about actual criminal cases? Something you have worked. I'll start." She told of her working the case involving Darrell Willis killing his girlfriend, Marie Chavez, in the woods and later moving her body to the dunes.

Both Jay Dee and T seemed impressed with that one.

"Your turn," Kat said to Jay Dee.

"Who's this Roxanne Abben? I'd like to meet her," said Jay Dee.

She'd like to meet you too, Kat thought and then said, "Go on, now. Your turn."

"Okay, but it's long and involved. Can't do it justice by shortening it," said Jay Dee.

"We have lots of time." Kat waved her right arm toward the road as a sign to carry on.

Jay Dee said, "There was this guy in the hill country with a massive spread between Marble Falls and Johnson City. His mom died and left it to him. This guy was a straight-up loser. Never had a job. He spent all his time online, gaming. He had a reputation as being a master online. But that wasn't paying the bills. He's squandered his inheritance and couldn't even pay the taxes on the land. So he devised a scheme to have these wannabe badasses to play Halo or some online game in real life. Guys would pay a thousand dollars each to hunt and kill one another. The winner would split the proceeds with this guy, Jed."

T sat up straighter, more interested in the story. "I heard about that."

"Yes, me too," said Kat. "Each time the local PD showed to bust him, they came up empty-handed; no evidence."

"Exactly," said Jay Dee. "He fed the dead bodies of the losers to his hogs."

"They'll do a number on the human body," said T.

"He must've had some inside information because when officers raided his place, he had sold the pig shit as fertilizer and was having a big ole barbecue for all the neighbors. Guess what was on the menu?"

"Pork," said Kat and T in unison.

"Got that right. So we tried a different approach. Took a while, but I got in as one of the players. Following the directions emailed from one of the dickhead gamers I'd previously busted for weed, I showed up with a grand in cash, a fake ID, and login info provided by my stoolie in exchange for not going to jail. We wanted this guy bad."

"You bust him on the spot?" asked Kat.

Jay Dee shook his head. "No evidence yet. I had to play along until I could nail this guy. He attached an anklet with some kind of transmitter to locate the dead bodies and also yellow ribbons you were supposed to take to provide evidence of your kills."

"How many other players?" asked T.

"A dozen, including me. We met at his cabin an hour before sunup. Shooting hours stared after sunrise, not before. When he said go, and I looked around, everyone was gone."

"What did you do?" Kat asked.

"I hauled ass. I had no choice. It all happened so quick that I didn't have a chance to do anything."

"That must have been scary," said T.

"Damn straight," said Jay Dee. "Once in the cover of the woods, I waited for the sun to rise. I could see a ravine to the west. The map showed that it ran back behind the cabin, so I followed, staying low. The shooting had already started."

"You really did this?" asked Kat, amazed.

"I had no choice. Do or die, if you know what I mean."

"Literally," said T.

"Once behind the cabin, I saw Jed come out with a rifle and some handheld electronic equipment. I figure it was a tracking device since he headed directly toward where I was hiding."

"Cheating bastard," said Kat.

"I was surrounded by eleven motherfuckers with weapons, and this guy was coming right at me. As I was about to stand up, identify myself, and put a stop to this nonsense, Jed points his rifle my way and fires. I heard something fall behind me."

"One of the eleven?" T asked.

"Yes. He must have seen me running and sneaked up behind me. I guess I should be grateful, but I knew this guy wasn't going to surrender, not now that I witnessed a murder, so I took off. He fired several times into the bushes, but I was already running low in the ravine."

"You are one lucky motherfucker," said Kat. "What happened next?"

"I knew that Jed's gunfire would surely draw attention, so I found a rock and climbed a tree."

"What was the rock for?" asked Kat.

"I smashed the transmitter locked around my ankle."

"Smart," T said.

"Not a moment too soon. I saw Jed walking right under the tree I was in. I watched him move off to the north. I climbed a little higher, and I could see a dead body on the edge of a pasture. Jed was going in that direction. I climbed down and ran like hell, trying to get ahead of him."

"Lucky no one else saw you, or you'd be a dead mother," T said.

"I know."

"Weren't you scared?" asked Kat.

"Not really. I was more focused than scared."

"More stupid than scared," T said.

"I located the dead body with the transmitter and found a crack in the rocks that gave me a good vantage point. Then I waited for Jed."

"A crack in the rocks sounds like a good place to get yourself trapped," said Kat.

"Just what I thought at the time but too late. Jed emerged from the woods to my left. He walked right by me, facing the victim. I put my rifle in the back of his neck and said, 'Drop it.'"

"He resist?" asked Kat

"He said that he wasn't a player. He was the sponsor, just out locating losers to dispose of the bodies. I told him who I was, informed him of his rights, and marched him off the property all the way to the highway. Other rangers were waiting. They moved in and rounded up the other players."

"So that was you. Wow," Kat said. "Impressive."

"Yep, that was me."

"Before we all bow down and kiss the ground you walk on," T said, "I have a case I worked down in Galveston."

"Let's hear," said Kat without hesitation.

T leaned forward, crossed his arms on the top of the front seat, and described his favorite case so far. "A guy was scamming people. He would hear about unsolved crimes that offered a reward, and he'd advertise a ridiculous amount of money for anyone providing information that led to solving the crime."

"Like Crime Stoppers," Kat said.

"Yes, but I'm talking tens of thousands of dollars. People would call his 800-number and tell him who committed the crime and where the criminal could be found. He would tell them to go to a locker at a train station, and he'd give them a locker number and combination. He would tell them to wait a week and then check the locker. If their info led to an arrest, the money would be there waiting. He would then call in the info to the real Crime Stoppers, collect the reward, and off he'd go."

"Nifty scam," said Jay Dee.

"Yeah, and the police really didn't mind; they got their cases solved and nobody got hurt. Just greedy people."

"So how does that top Jay Dee?" asked Kat.

"Patience, my dear, patience. I'm getting to that," T said, smiling. "Seems this guy wasn't just local. He made his way up to New York and ran his scam several times. One such tip helped put away a hit man for the mob."

"Interesting," said Kat. "Did the mob retaliate?"

"In a way," said T. "He knew he needed to lay low after that. He changed his identity; moved to Galveston."

"How'd they find him?" Jay Dee asked.

"This, sports fans, is where it gets real. Seems one of this guy's informants was a police officer, one of New York's finest. He had all the information on a mob hit, but saw the chance to make some serious coins and still get the bad guy. Once he realized he had been scammed, he was one PO'ed PO."

Kat laughed. "Good one. Can I use that?"

"Most certainly," said T. "Just be sure to give credit where credit is due."

"How does this police officer fit in?" asked Jay Dee.

"He had the means to track this guy down. For a price, he let the mob know the scammer was cooling it, Galveston way. Ba-da-bing, ba-da-boom—scammer washes ashore one fine afternoon. Not a pretty sight. The ocean life was provided a buffet, and everyone took a bite. Sharks, fish, crab—this guy was so decomposed it was hard to see how he died, but an x-ray showed a ten-penny nail lodged midbrain."

"Ouch!" said Kat. "Don't see that every day."

"Tell me about it," Jay Dee said.

"They shot him through the mouth with a nail gun. They could have left the body in the house to make it look like a suicide, but—"

"They wanted to send a message," Kat said.

"Got that right,'" T said. "I took that nail, collected at the autopsy, to be analyzed."

"Get a hit?" asked Jay Dee.

"Affirmative," said T. "Apparently some mob guys in New Jersey also worked construction. They liked using the tools of the trade. Unlike my friend here, I can shorten the story, 'cause I gotta whiz."

"Me too," Jay Dee said.

"Y'all pregnant?" asked Kat. "We'll never get home, stopping at every little town so you ladies can take a piss."

"It's been three hours," T said, "but back to the case. After months of intensive investigation, we arrested the two guys who killed the scammer and the PO who gave them his whereabouts."

Jay Dee pulled the cruiser into the parking lot of a convenience store. Kat saw a sign on the window advertising boiled Cajun peanuts.

"All right!" she said. "Y'all want some spicy peanuts?"

"Never tried 'em," Jay Dee said.

"The first guy to eat a coconut took a chance," T said. "What the hell—I'll try, but at this moment I have more pressing matters, and by pressing, I mean the inside of my bladder." T ran past Jay Dee and Kat.

"Moves pretty good for a big boy," Kat said.

"You should have seen him on a football field, before the accident, I mean."

"I wouldn't want to try to block him; that's for sure," Kat said.

Jay Dee looked quizzically at Kat. "You know football?"

Kat laughed. "Hell, man, I'm the youngest with four older brothers. Besides, I'm from Alice, where football is king. Our motto is, It's not how big the dog is in the fight but how big the fight is in the dog. Yes, I know football."

"Nice."

Once they were back in the car, Kat said to T, "I like that saying about the coconut. Do you mind if I use it in one of my stories?"

"You write?" T asked. "Awesome; me too. What do you write?"

"Short stories mostly. Some poetry."

"Me too. Well, not the poetry. I love short stories. Enough with these cases. Tell us one of your stories, Kat."

Jay Dee waved his left hand toward the road, mimicking Kat's gesture of hours before. "We got lots of time. Let's hear a story."

While munching on boiled peanuts, Kat began. "There was this professor at a small college in Louisiana. He was married to one of his former students, and one day he decided to cancel his afternoon class so he could knock off with some afternoon delight."

"I love afternoon delight," T said.

"Too much information," Kat said. "Who's telling this story anyway?"

"Sorry," said T.

"When he got home that afternoon, he went to the bedroom … and saw his naked wife underneath some guy. He couldn't see the guy's face, just his ass pounding the wife."

"What did he do?" asked T.

"Patience, dear sir, patience. I'm getting to that. He did nothing. He left and went back to his office."

"I'd have killed that motherfucker," T said, "and her too."

"Well, he knew that the husband was always the first suspect, so that was out of the question. He was a creative-writing professor, so he made this an assignment for his students—to come up with a method of killing a spouse with no clues leading back to the murder."

"Ingenious!" T said. "I like this guy."

"The professor read all the submitted papers and was dismayed by all of them. Then one of his students, a low achiever, came to his office. Without being asked, the student walked inside, closed the door behind him, and took a seat. The professor was annoyed—this was a student who hadn't turned in the assignment. So the student says, 'That's what I want to talk about. I don't want there to be any record of this, but this is how I would do it.' The student lays out a plan for the spouse to have a scuba diving accident in Mexico. Apparently, it happens all the time, and no one suspects anything. The professor still doesn't get it; he insists he needs a paper turned in so he can give the kid a grade.

"So the student says, 'The grade's an A for the course, but it's not a story; it's a plan. I can make this happen.'"

"Cocky SOB," said Jay Dee.

Kat nodded. "The student then said, 'Take out life insurance on both of you. I get an A for your course. You get rid of a wife and become rich to boot. Win/win.' The professor was now intrigued, so the student laid out every step. The professor agrees to the plan and waits for its fruition."

"*Fruition*. I like that word," T said. "I might start using it in my writing."

"You have my permission," Kat said.

"Just give credit where credit is due," Jay Dee added.

"May I finish?" Kat asked.

"Please," the men said in unison.

"The professor gets a call from Mexico. He can barely make out the broken English, but he did understand the message that his wife was dead. Now his only worry was that the student would later try to blackmail him, so the professor hatched a plan to ensure that didn't happen. He once went with a colleague down a back road to Lake Pontchartrain. His friend's dog had died, and the guy fed the remains to the alligators. The gators made a quick meal of the animal. So the professor had the student come over the evening he returned from Mexico. They celebrated over a glass of wine, but the student's drink was laced with Rohypnol.

"The professor took the unconscious student to the place where the gators ate the dog. He brought along pieces of dead chickens to entice the gators. He dragged the kid's limp body near the edge of the water. He started throwing chicken pieces into the water, and when the gators arrived, he reached down to grab the student … only to have a bright light shone directly into his eyes, which knocked him off balance and backward a bit."

"The police?" Jay Dee asked.

"No, that's when the professor heard a familiar voice—his *wife's* voice—asking, 'What's going on here?' The professor said, 'I thought you were dead. I got a call from the medical examiner in Mexico.' The wife said, 'Amazing what a hundred bucks buys you in Mexico. No, I'm not dead. And you remember that guy you saw me fucking? That's him,' and she pointed to the still-unconscious student. The professor was so stunned that without realizing it, he'd backed into the water, and the gators had cut off any exit to land."

"Hot damn," said T. "The wife gets the insurance money and can keep her fuck buddy too. I just love a good twist."

For the remainder of the trip, T and Kat took turns telling stories.

Jay Dee listened, impressed with their creativity, and finally said, "I wouldn't want either of you two plotting to kill me."

73

Kat asked Jay Dee to pull over in the next town.

"My house is just minutes away," he said, "and I promise it's a lot cleaner than you will find around here."

Kat agreed. "I can wait a few minutes."

Jay Dee turned down a dead-end road. The terrain changed drastically from what was common for the area. "This is called Roller Coaster Road," Jay Dee said.

"I can see why." Kat felt her stomach go up into her chest when Jay Dee topped one of the many hills a little too fast. "I just hope the ride ends soon."

Jay Dee pulled into a long, wide concrete driveway that led to a small house. Kat could see the lights of the harbor bridge across the bay.

"We're close to Corpus," she said, exiting the vehicle.

Jay Dee opened the front door for her. "The bathroom's to the right. We'll wait here."

Kat was through the tiny living room in a flash and quickly spotted her goal. Once she finished relieving herself, she took her time before going back outside. She looked around and saw a small, tidy kitchen with two fish prints hanging on the wall. She recognized one as a large speckled trout and the other as a much larger redfish.

Kat turned to face the rear of the house. The entire back wall was glass, and the twinkling of lights on the bridge leading into Corpus were amazing. The water below was still, and the lights' reflection appeared to be painted on its surface.

"What a view," she said, walking out the front door. "This place yours?"

"My parents," Jay Dee said, locking the front door. "We would come down here from Floresville every chance we got. I love this place."

"Me too," T said, stretching. "I declare myself officially off duty. Got any beer?"

"As much as you want," said Jay Dee, "but we need to return this cruiser first. How about we come back afterward and knock back some cold ones and fish off the pier."

"I'm game," said T.

"I have plans," Kat said. "Thanks, though. I saw some nice fish prints in there."

"My mom did those. She does good work. We caught those off the pier. Are you sure you can't come back?"

"I would if I could—believe me. I have plans with a dear friend—a prima donna but a good friend all the same."

"Well, bring Donna, and you two come fish," Jay Dee suggested.

"Another time, I hope," Kat said.

Kat dropped off T and Jay Dee and exchanged the bulky cruiser for her dependable Mustang. She wasted no time in calling Roxanne, "We still on for tonight?"

"I thought I was going to have to start without you." Roxanne giggled. "Oh wait—I did actually."

"Are you wasted already?"

"Define *wasted*."

"Damn, guess we're staying in tonight."

"We're going out," said Roxanne, slurring her words.

Kat played out her options in her head: *Cancel, and go fishing with the guys. No, Roxanne would never forgive me for that. Take Roxanne fishing with the guys. Nope, not letting her near Jay Dee, especially when she has had a few drinks. Go out to a club with a drunk Roxanne. Not a good option either. I'd be alone as soon as the first pretty boy walked by. Looks like we're having our own private party. Damn.*

Roxanne handed Kat a glass of wine the instant she walked through the door.

Kat took a long sip. "Hmm, this is good. What is it?"

"Merlot. Coppala." Roxanne pointed to an almost-empty bottle. "Don't worry, doll. I got two more once this is gone."

Kat drank the rest of the wine in her glass in one gulp and poured the remainder of the bottle into her glass.

Roxanne opened another one. "How was Huntsville?"

"Actually, it was a good trip. Met a professor who is a blood-spatter expert. He confirmed several things that I'd suspected all along."

"Such as?"

"That the shots were fired from the back seat."

"Aguilar is not going to be happy to hear that."

"Fuck him," said Kat, taking another drink. "I'm not so sure he didn't do those two and is trying to make it appear that they shot each other. He's having the new guys address him as *Captain*."

"Motive, possibly," Roxanne said, "but where's your proof?"

"The professor, Dr. Nash, said whoever fired the shots would have blood spots on their clothing, especially the shirt."

"Did Aguilar have blood on his? You were there."

"His shirt was clean, but he could have changed before he called it in."

"Stretching it a bit, doll. Here—let me pour you another. Tell me more about this Jay Dee."

75

Kat figured the guys could tell she was wearing the same clothes as yesterday, but she didn't really care. As she entered the office, both T and Jay Dee rose to greet her.

"Catch any fish?" she asked.

"We decided to stop off at a bar instead," said T. "Met a few of Corpus's finest. Good guys."

As if on cue, two fellow police officers appeared at the door, holding Starbucks coffee. Kat recognized the faces but couldn't recall their names.

They shook hands with Jay Dee and T and offered them coffee. Kat noticed they did neither to her.

"Made an impression, I see," Kat said as the officers departed.

"We had a few drinks, told some stories, had some laughs," T said, offering Kat his coffee.

"Stories, huh?" Kat accepted the coffee as if it was a shrine. "Same ones you told me yesterday?"

"Naw, we got lots of different ones," T said as Jay Dee nursed his coffee.

"Okay, let's hear what it takes to get patrol to bring Starbucks," Kat said.

Jay Dee took another sip, set his cup down, and joined the conversation. "I told them about the time T and I got our boat hung up on an underwater stump about twenty feet from the bank."

"How does that happen?" Kat asked.

"Well, I was driving the motor, and T was sitting up front watching for stumps and underwater longs. I couldn't see around him, and we got the boat so stuck we couldn't get it off. I took a four-foot paddle and acted like I was hitting the bottom of the lake about three feet down."

"Yes, he tricked me," T said. "I thought it was so shallow that I just slipped over the edge."

"How deep was it?" Kat asked

"I don't know," said T. "All I know is that I went under about fifteen feet before I realized it, and I still didn't touch bottom. I hadn't taken a deep breath because I thought I'd only be waist deep. I almost drowned trying to swim up to the surface—moss was hanging all over me. I tell you I was scared."

"I got scared too. I figured we were only that far from shore." Jay Dee pointed at the wall of Captain Moore's office. "So how deep could it be?"

Kat noticed Aguilar looking up from behind his desk in Captain Moore's office. She egged T on. "I'm guessing you didn't drown, but why were you in front of Jay Dee in the first place? I would figure it would have been the other way around."

"Funny you asked," said Jay Dee. "We were fishing again in my dad's jon boat, a fourteen-footer with a 9.5 horsepower Evinrude."

Kat nodded as if she understood.

"T was in the front, paddling, scaring the fish. I asked him to switch places so I could paddle."

"He told me, not asked me," said T. "Said I wasn't quiet enough, so I should go to the back of the boat. He started paddling but still didn't catch any fish."

Jay Dee rolled his eyes. "It was hot, midday, so when I saw a break in the woods, I told T to start the motor and take us through the clearing."

"I said, No way, Jose," T interrupted.

"Why?" Kat asked.

"I remembered a time when I was driving my brother-in-law's ski boat on the river, and I was gonna be cool by running full speed up to a sandbar, kill the motor, and coast up beside the other boats."

"Didn't it turn out as planned?" Kat asked.

"I waited too late to kill the motor and beached the whole boat. I said that I would never drive a boat again."

"I get the feeling you drove another boat again," said Kat.

"Jay Dee said, 'It's easy, not like a speed boat,' so I pulled the cord to start the motor."

Jay Dee hopped off the corner of the desk where he'd been sitting and became animated. "Everything was going good, and then we started picking up speed. I look up ahead, and we were headed straight for a huge tree in the middle of the clearing. I turned back to look at T, and all I saw was the back of his head."

"You weren't looking where you were going?" Kat asked T.

"I was trying everything I could to stop the motor. I was pushing buttons and turning the handle."

"We were going full speed, straight for the tree," said Jay Dee. "I started moving toward the back when we hit the damn tree head-on. I went flying almost out of the boat; the motor was still wide open, running full throttle. We were wedged against the tree. It dented the front of my dad's boat."

"What did your dad say?" Kat asked.

"He didn't let us take out his boat after that," said Jay Dee, "but he wasn't mad."

Turning to T, Kat said, "You said 'the' river. You only have one river in Arkansas?"

"We have plenty of rivers," said T. "Buffalo—first national river, by the way."

"White River," said Jay Dee. "Good fishing."

"Mulberry, Ouachita," T continued.

"I get it," Kat interrupted. "So all you Arkansas boys know how to spin yarns?"

"Yarns are for women," said T with a grin. "We men tell stories."

"Tall tales, if you ask me," Kat said.

"No, ma'am, real life; better than fiction," T said. "There was this fella from Little Rock. He came down to Redfield to visit a cousin. All the boys were sitting around the fire, drinking beer, telling jokes. We'd tell the same jokes so often that we gave each joke a number. Instead of telling the whole thing, somebody would yell out a number, and we'd think of the joke and laugh as though it was the first time we heard it. Well, this new fella, not wanting to be left out, decides to call out a number, but nobody laughs."

"That number wasn't a funny joke?" Kat asked.

"Nope. Some people can tell jokes, and some people can't," said T as he left the room.

Kat turned to Jay Dee. "Is he for real?" Before Jay Dee could answer, Kat's phone rang. "Detective Gonzales," she said.

"Kitten," said Ric, "got a DB out in Petronila. Doesn't look right. Thought you should take a look."

"I'm meeting with the chief in a few," replied Kat, "but I'll send the rangers, Jay Dee Baker and T … uh Terrance Jones. Address?"

Jay Dee handed Kat a notepad and pen. She wrote down the information, tore off the top sheet, and handed it to T as he came back into the room. "Ric is the chief investigator for the ME. He said something looks off with a DB. You guys check it out, please."

"Roger that," said T.

Kat walked to the door, stopped, and said, without looking back, "And don't call me Roger."

76

"You don't have an appointment," said Juanita.

"I know," said Kat as she breezed by the chief's secretary and straight into the office, knocking as she opened the door.

"What now?" asked Chief Gibson.

"I had a blood-spatter expert look at the photos of Detectives Timms and Huerta. He said the shooter was in the back seat. They did *not* shoot each other, like Aguilar is claiming."

"What expert?" asked the chief.

"Dr. Graham Nash, a professor at—"

"Sam Houston. I know who he is."

"He also said that the shooter would be covered in blood from back spatter. Chief, I think Javier may be covering up something."

"What the hell are you saying?" yelled the chief.

Kat, unruffled, continued. "I think Detective Aguilar may have been the shooter. He could have shot them both to make sure he was the one to replace Captain Moore. I want to get a warrant to search his cruiser and his home. It's the only way to know for sure."

"Get out of my office—now. Don't come back with any more bullshit about getting a warrant, or I'll send you back to patrol so fast you'll—"

Kat was out the door before the chief finished his sentence.

77

In the elevator going down, Kat called Joel. "Hey, I need a favor, and don't ask why; just do it."

"Are you asking me to break the law?" said Joel.

"No, nothing like that," said Kat. "You know where Detective Aguilar lives?"

"Can't say that I do. ID and PD don't hang out together."

"Poenisch. Corner of Alameda and Poenisch; house number 501. I believe the trash gets picked up there today. Can you and Brenda grab his trash out by the curb and bring it back to the lab?"

"I guess so. We're slow at the moment before all the businesses open and find out they've been broken into over the weekend. What are we looking for?"

"Tell you when you get back. I'll meet you in the lab."

Kat went back to her desk to allow the two ID techs a chance to retrieve Aguilar's trash. She was surprised to see T and Jay Dee still there.

"I thought you would be …" She trailed off as T pointed toward Captain Moore's office. The door opened, and Javier Aguilar stepped out.

"Detective Gonzales, come into my office."

"Good news travels fast," Kat mumbled as she walked past Jay Dee and T. Kat closed the door behind her upon entering the office.

"I just received a call from Chief Gibson informing me of your intentions of serving me, a fellow officer, with a warrant to search my property. I can't believe the gall. You think I would murder my best friends for a job? That scares me. It makes me wonder what kind of person you are." Kat started to speak but Aguilar cut her off. "I'm not through. You have never been a team player here—always a loner, trying to grab the spotlight for yourself. If we weren't so short-handed I'd suspend you without pay, indefinitely. I'm the interim captain, not you. You don't make assignments; that's my job. Understood?"

Looking Aguilar straight in the eyes, Kat replied, "Yes, sir. Is that all, sir?"

"No, it's not all. Where did you think you were sending those two outside?" He nodded toward T and Jay Dee. "Petronila is county. Let county handle it."

"They did," said Kat. "They are calling it a suicide, but the ME's investigator doesn't see it that way. I thought the Rangers could go. That way we won't be stepping on anyone's toes."

"Run that by me next time. You are on thin ice. Tread lightly. You can go, but send the Rangers in here."

"Yes, sir." She left the office and bee-lined it up to the crime lab. "Sorry, fellas," she said as she passed T and Jay Dee. "The man needs to see you in his office."

Jay Dee and T entered Aguilar's office, leaving the door open behind them.

"I need you two to check out the call, but do so as Rangers, not representatives of Corpus PD. Sheriff's deputy says suicide, but we want to be sure. Understood?"

"Loud and clear, Captain," said T as both men nodded and exited the room.

79

Ric was waiting outside when T and Jay Dee arrived. After cordial introductions, Ric asked both men, "Have you worked many suicides?"

"More than I care to," replied Jay Dee.

"Yeah, me too," said T.

"How many have you seen with the body lying supine when the victim pulled the trigger?" Ric asked.

"Not very many. Most were sitting or standing when they ended their lives," said T.

"I agree," said Jay Dee, "although I have seen some lying down."

"Did those shoot themselves in the temple?" Ric asked.

Jay Dee contemplated the question. "No, not a one. They all shot themselves up through the mouth."

"Well, get ready to add to your experience. Either we have an unusual suicide, or someone else pulled the trigger."

"The wife?" asked T.

"Not my job," said Ric. "That's why I called you."

"Let's take a look," said Jay Dee. "Anyone home?"

"The wife," said Ric. "Elizabeth Wesson, forty-seven. She volunteers at the kids' school, or did until they died two weeks ago. Twin boys, sixteen years old. Rolled the truck they were driving. Both intoxicated. Sad."

"Whoa, man," said T. "This woman has lost her sons and her husband. Any other family here?"

"No, she's all alone."

Jay Dee knocked on the door. It opened slightly, and a tall, redheaded woman peered through the crack.

"Mrs. Wesson, I'm Jay Dee Baker, and this is my partner, Terrance Jones. We are Texas Rangers, ma'am, sent here to make sure you are okay. May we come inside?"

The door opened wide, revealing a slim woman wearing an apron over a blue dress and house shoes. "Of course, please do come in. Can I make you gentlemen some coffee?"

"Yes, black, thank you," said Jay Dee, trying to keep Mrs. Wesson occupied and out of their way.

Ric showed T and Jay Dee the way to Mr. Wesson, still lying in the bed where he was shot. "I see what you mean," said T as he inspected the body. "It appears the bullet entered at the left temple and exited the right side through the mastoid process."

"Very odd," said Jay Dee. "Most people taking their own lives aim the gun upward, toward the brain. This angle was downward. Good eye, Ric."

"Stiletto marking indicates the barrel was in direct contact," said T.

"Yes, that fits with suicide," said Ric, "but the angle is giving me pause."

"Let's talk with the wife," said Jay Dee. "Maybe she will shed some light."

The three men returned to the living room just as Mrs. Wesson appeared, carrying a silver tray with a coffeepot and four cups of fine china. T helped her with the tray, setting it down on the coffee table in front of them.

"Thank you," said Mrs. Wesson as she began pouring coffee into the cups. "Cream, sugar?" she asked. When she'd finished, she sat in a small rocking chair, facing them.

The men took a sip from their respective cups. "Um, good coffee, Mrs. Wesson," said Jay Dee.

"Elizabeth," she said. "Please call me Elizabeth."

"Elizabeth," Jay Dee said. "I'm very sorry for your loss—your husband and your children. Do you have relatives in the area?"

"No, we were originally from Detroit. My husband is a lawyer—or was. He won a huge settlement. Large enough for us to relocate. We had visited Corpus Christi on a vacation and just fell in love with the water. Hank, my husband, didn't want to live in the city, so we bought this place. Been here ever since."

"How long ago was that?" asked T.

"Four years. The kids were in sixth grade when we came down. They were sophomores at Tuloso-Midway this year ..."

"How did your husband handle the death of your boys?" asked Jay Dee.

"He was furious. He wanted the owner of the liquor store prosecuted for selling them alcohol. He called every law enforcement agency, even your office in Austin. They investigated but said there was no evidence to determine where they got the Crown."

"Crown Royal?" asked T.

"Yes," replied Elizabeth.

"How did they know your boys were drinking Crown Royal?" asked T.

"There was a bottle still in the truck," said Ric. "Almost empty. Their blood alcohol levels were over 1.2. Doesn't take much for thin sixteen-year-olds to become intoxicated."

Elizabeth started to say something but then stopped herself.

"What is it, Elizabeth?" Jay Dee asked.

"I guess it really doesn't matter now, now that Hank is dead," she said.

"Go on," urged Jay Dee.

"Hank was so upset that nothing would happen to those bastards, as he called the liquor store people, that he followed the owner home one night after work and pulled a gun on the man. It scared the old man so bad he had a heart attack and died in the ambulance on the way to the hospital. Hank confessed to me. He said he just wanted to talk to the old guy. Try to scare a confession out of him with the gun. Didn't plan for him to die, not then anyway."

"When did this happen?" asked T.

"Last night," said Ric.

"Yes," said Elizabeth. "Hank came home so upset. He needed a drink to steady his nerves. That's when he saw it."

"Saw what?" asked Jay Dee.

"I keep a tidy house. A maid comes every week for mopping and dusting, but we don't allow her behind the bar. 'Don't want the help drinking the booze' said Hank."

"What did Hank see?" Jay Dee asked.

"He saw the dust surrounding the spot where his bottle of Crown used to be," said Elizabeth.

All three men drew back. "So you think that's why he killed himself?" asked T.

"Yes, our children were our life."

"Did you go back behind the bar too?" asked Jay Dee.

"No, never," said Elizabeth. "I couldn't bear it."

"This is good coffee, Elizabeth. Got anything sweet to eat? Cookies, maybe?" asked Jay Dee.

"I have some cookie dough in the freezer. The boys had to sell it for a fundraiser at school. I'll make a batch." And with that, she went into the kitchen.

"Do we have an electrostatic lifter in the cruiser?" Jay Dee asked T.

"Probably not, but I'll look," said T.

"The crime scene van is not far away. They should have one," offered Ric.

"Call 'em," said Jay Dee.

80

The crime scene van pulled up five minutes later. Ric made the introductions. The tech handed T the case containing the device. "You know how to use it?" asked the tech.

"Yep, shocked myself enough times to make sure I have a good ground," said T. "Be right back."

Ric joined Jay Dee and T as they returned to the house. They rolled out a single sheet of Mylar three feet long and one foot wide. "Shiny side up," said Jay Dee, making sure T placed the black side down on the floor behind the bar.

"I got this," said T. "You just sit tight and hook up the ground, shiny side down."

Jay Dee complied, and T turned on the device.

"I've never seen one in action," said Ric.

"The electrostatic lifter charges this sheet of Mylar with a negative charge," T explained. "That causes any dust particles underneath to become attached to the dark side. We use this roller to make sure we achieve as much contact as possible with whatever is on the floor." After forty-five seconds, T turned off the switch. "Let's see what we have here," T said as he turned over the Mylar.

Two small footprints made of light color from the dust stood in contrast to the black background.

"Those look like they could be from the wife," said Ric.

"Yes, but it's not enough by itself," said Jay Dee. "Hand it to me, T, and you fellas stay out of sight."

Jay Dee took the Mylar into the kitchen. "Elizabeth, I need you to see something." He turned the footprints over for her to view. "We found these footprints behind the bar. Looks like a match to those slippers you're wearing. We can find out for sure back at the lab. You told us that you never went behind the bar."

Elizabeth started to protest, but Jay Dee cut her off. He pulled her toward the bedroom where her dead husband lay. "You know, Elizabeth, thieves have the technology now to come along behind you in the grocery store and wave heat-sensing infrared scanners over the key pad to determine your PIN."

"Yes, yes, I've read about that," said Elizabeth. "You're supposed to touch all the numbers when your transaction is complete."

"That's exactly right," said Jay Dee. "Thieves are always coming up with different ways to cheat people, and law enforcement is continuing to adapt to thwart their attempts. We use infrared technology too. You see, people give off heat that's invisible to the naked eye."

"So you can use that to determine where people have been too." Elizabeth nodded as Jay Dee turned to face her. "I shot him. I'm sorry. I'm the one who saw the missing bottle. Something inside snapped. I couldn't bear to look at him, knowing that he was the reason my children are dead. I asked him to keep it locked away. I just couldn't take it." Tears rolled down her face.

Listening in, Ric whispered to T, "We don't have that type of technology."

"He didn't say we did; she said it. Everything Jay Dee said was true. He just pointed her in the right direction, and she made the leap."

"You boys are good," Ric said.

T smiled, tilted his head, and accepted the compliment.

81

Kat waited anxiously for Joel to return with Aguilar's trash. She knew no warrant was needed since his trash would be out by the street. When they arrived, Joel was carrying two large black garbage bags, and Brenda had one large and one small bag.

"What are we looking for?" asked Brenda.

"Better for me if I don't say, but if it's there, you will know it when you see it," Kat said.

"Which one you want to start with?" asked Joel.

"You pick," said Kat. "I'm just an observer."

"I'm going with the small bag," said Brenda. "The other felt like a bunch of beer cans." She undid the twist tie used to close the bag and pulled the top open and down, revealing a white shirt.

"What do we have here?" asked Joel.

Using gloved hands, Brenda removed the shirt and laid it face up on some brown butcher paper that Joel had set out on the table. "Looks like blood," said Brenda.

"Yes, and lots of it," said Joel.

All three saw the JAA monogram on the bloodstained shirt at the same time. Kat knew that Aguilar's middle name was Almos because she'd seen his initials on every shirt he wore, and she once asked him about it. His mother's maiden name, she recalled him saying.

Joel and Brenda looked at Kat in disbelief.

"Can you run those blood samples? See if we get a match?" Kat asked.

"How did you know?" asked Joel.

"I didn't," said Kat, "but I had my suspicions."

"I'll get right on it," said Joel. "Call you as soon as the results come in."

Kat wanted to ask Joel and Brenda to keep quiet about what they were doing but thought better about it. *News spreads fast through these walls.* "Thank you," she said and left.

It wasn't even noon, but Kat knew her drinking buddy would be up for the task. Kat needed to celebrate, and a cold beer while sitting on Roxanne's back porch, watching the river pass by, would be a good start. Besides, she didn't want to be in the building once the word spread of finding Detective Javier Almos Aguilar's bloodstained shirt in his trash.

"Why didn't he burn it?" Brenda asked as she was leaving.

"With this drought, the whole county is in a burn ban," replied Joel.

82

On her way to Roxanne's, Kat's phone rang. It was Jay Dee.

"You okay? We couldn't help hearing Aguilar this morning. He was coming on pretty loud."

"All's well," replied Kat. "I think he's worried."

"About his job?" asked Jay Dee.

"That, among other things," said Kat. "How'd it go in Petronila?"

"The wife confessed," he said.

"Oh, you walk in like you're a priest, and she spills her guts." Kat laughed.

"Something like that," said Jay Dee.

"Tell me all about it tomorrow. I'm taking the afternoon off. Can you boys handle things?"

"Sure; see you tomorrow."

Kat called Roxanne to inform her that she was giving both of them the day off. Minutes later, Kat pulled into Roxanne's driveway and drove under the house built on stilts to accommodate the common flooding of the Nueces River. She saw Roxanne on the front porch.

"Already put two in the freezer," Roxanne called to her. "Come on up. I have some tequila from my trip to Mexico that I want you to try—smooth."

"When did you go to Mexico?" Kat asked.

"Last week. Had a blast."

"Where'd you go?"

"Puerto Vallarta."

"With who?"

"It's with *whom*, and I'm not telling."

"I can't believe you left the country without telling me, and worse, not telling me with whom you went. That's asking for trouble."

"Spur of the moment. He asked; I said yes. Here—try this." Roxanne poured the clear liquid into two shot glasses from a turquoise bottle with a picture of a whale breaching on the label. "Sip; don't shoot it. It's Arrecife. Two hundred dollars a bottle but worth every penny, or at least every one of his pennies."

"What's in the bottom of the glasses?" Kat asked.

"Agave plant. All hand-blown glass. Cool, huh?"

They clicked their glasses together, but before Roxanne took a sip, she stopped to ask, "What are we toasting? You didn't say on the phone."

"Let's just toast to the stylish monogrammed shirts of one Javier Almos Aguilar." Kat took a sip. "Oh my God, this is good—very good. Now tell me about your trip. Puerto Vallarta, huh?"

The two spent the remainder of the afternoon drinking and sharing details about Roxanne's trip and Kat's morning. Kat needed to unwind and felt safe in doing so in present company.

83

The following morning Kat checked her messages. She had three, one of which was from Joel: "Blood types on the shirt are congruent with the types belonging to Timms and Huerta. Won't have results from DNA until forty-eight hours. Will let you know."

The second message was from Chief Gibson: "I need to see you in my office, right away."

The last message came from Detective Aguilar: "I don't know why you are doing this, but I can tell you it won't work. If you want this job so bad that you're willing to frame a fellow peace officer, then fuck you."

"Looking forward to another day in paradise," Kat said as she stepped into her shower. She weighed her options as the water ran over her body. She decided to call in sick. She was sick of work after all. Not the job; she loved police work. She just hated all the crap that went with it, like the chief and Aguilar. "Think I'll head over to Alice," she said, as though speaking to the showerhead.

84

T and Jay Dee both felt Kat's absence at work.

"Think she got fired, or maybe put on suspension?" T asked.

"Out of our hands, buddy," Jay Dee replied. "I'll give her a call later to see what's up."

Captain Aguilar motioned for the two to enter his office. "We have a suspect in custody. Could be a serial rapist we've been after, going on two years. Fits the MO. He breaks into houses of young girls who are home alone or babysitting. Wears a ski mask to cover his face, gloves, and a condom that he takes with him. Informed enough to not leave evidence. He uses a knife to force himself on the victims."

"What makes you think this guy is the one?" asked T.

"Nothing that we can take to court. We caught him sneaking along the bay. There was a break-in last night not far from where we picked him up."

"What happened, exactly?" asked Jay Dee.

"Fourteen-year-old babysitter was on the phone with her mom. Kids were asleep in their rooms. Girl sees a shadow move in the kitchen and tells her mom. Mom yells to Dad and calls 911. The girl yells at the kitchen, saying she's called the cops and that she has a gun and knows how to use it. Guy runs off."

"He brought a knife to a gunfight," said T. "Did she see him?"

"No, only shadows, but the dad lives next door. He came running with a shotgun. Said he saw a masked figure wearing dark clothes run out the side garage door and down toward the bay. Too far away to shoot with a shotgun."

"Cool head for a fourteen-year-old," said Jay Dee. "You said he broke in? How?"

"Appears to have jimmied the lock on the side door leading into the garage. Easy access to the house from there; leads right into the kitchen."

"ID still on the scene?" asked Jay Dee.

"No, this all transpired last night around ten thirty. They'll be going back this morning to perform another search in the daylight; see if they missed anything."

"Perfect. We'll head that way. Got the address?" asked Jay Dee.

Aguilar looked at his notes. "It's 1511 Doddridge. Go south on Ocean Drive, which turns into Shoreline. Turn right at the light. You'll see it on the corner, right side. ID should be on their way also. Let me know what you come up with. I want to nail this bastard."

It took T and Jay Dee less than ten minutes to arrive. The crime scene van pulled in right behind them. Jay Dee met the driver before he could exit the van. "I'm Ranger Baker, and that is Ranger Jones. Detective Aguilar asked us to help with the search. We've been—"

"I know," the driver interrupted. "I heard about you guys. Glad to have you onboard. I'm Joel Garza." He stepped out of the van, opened the side door, and grabbed what looked like a fishing tackle box. T and Jay Dee recognized it as the crime scene kit.

"Got Mikrosil in there?" asked Jay Dee.

"Sure do," replied Joel. "Planning to use it on the point of entry?"

"Yes," said Jay Dee. Turning to T, he said, "Why don't you take a look around the windows. Perp had to look inside to make sure nobody else was home."

When they reached the side door of the garage, Jay Dee and Joel could see several scratches in the wood and the metal portion around the latch.

"I'm going to make two separate coverings. You do the scratches in the wood, and I'll take the metal," said Joel as he handed Jay Dee two note cards. Joel then took a toothpaste-size tube and made a two-inch line down each card. He took a smaller tube that held the hardener and made another line beside each of the first two. He handed Jay Dee a popsicle stick, and Jay Dee gave Joel one of the note cards. Each man mixed the two lines together using the wooden stick. Joel then transferred his mixture to the metal, covering it entirely. In turn, Jay Dee transferred his to cover the scratches in the wooden frame.

"Glad to see you use the gray," said Jay Dee.

"Yeah, the white doesn't give enough contrast under the scope," said Joel. "Should be ready in about ten minutes, but in this humidity, I'll give it fifteen. I'll stick around here if you want to assist your partner."

Jay Dee left and walked around the back of the house. He saw T backing out of a huge oleander.

"I knocked; no answer," said T. "Don't want to spook anyone inside by looking through a window unannounced."

"I knew you would," said Jay Dee. "Got anything?"

"Got footprints there," T said, pointing toward the ground in front of a window. "Tennis shoes; not much to go on, though. Prints on top of prints. Bet he stayed here awhile."

"He had good cover."

"Exactly. I'm going to collect pollen samples. The perp's clothes has to have been covered by pollen from this bush. Might take time, but we can get a match."

"Palynography?" asked Jay Dee.

T smiled. "Got that right. Even plants have unique DNA. I'll use dental stone on the footprints anyway. You never know—might see details we can use. I need some bags to collect the pollen."

T and Jay Dee made their way back to the garage to check on Joel.

"Still tacky," said Joel. "Probably another five minutes."

"Got any small polyvinyl bags in there?" T pointed to the crime scene kit. "I need to collect some pollen samples."

"I only have the gallon size," said Joel. "But I have some paper. You can make a druggist fold."

"Show me," said T.

Joel took out three sheets of white notebook paper and handed one each to T and Jay Dee. "Fold over, hamburger-style." He demonstrated as he spoke. T and Jay Dee followed, folding their paper in half. "Now trifold." The two other men followed suit. "One last fold upward, and you can tuck the lip into the bottom. Voila—a druggist fold. You can safely transport powder, diamonds, even pollen."

"Thanks," said T. "Didn't learn that one in school."

"Me either," said Jay Dee. "I had heard about it but was never taught how to do it. So simple. Thanks."

"No problem," said Joel. "There's always a sheet of paper somewhere. Kat is the one who taught me. She learned it at Del Mar."

"Been wondering where she is," said Jay Dee. "You heard from her recently?"

"I talked with her yesterday. Told her the blood evidence matched, but DNA wouldn't be back until tomorrow."

T and Jay Dee both looked at each other. T turned back to Joel. "What DNA evidence?"

Joel told them about the shirt they'd found in Aguilar's trash. "The blood types match those of Timms and Huerta."

"Holy smoke, Batman," said T. "That's why she went off the reservation. She's waiting on the results of the DNA."

"I tend to agree," said Jay Dee. "But we have a perp in custody, and this evidence is not going to collect itself. Let's see if it's ready."

Joel touched the back of the Mikrosil. "Feels ready," he said and then gently began pulling on the side. Once removed from the frame, he turned it over to show Jay Dee. "Lots of good marking there."

Jay Dee nodded in approval. "Check the other one."

The lift from the metal was equally successful.

"Awesome," said Jay Dee. "Can you take these back to the lab, get the perp's knife, and make some exemplars to see if he used his knife to enter the garage? I'll help T collect the pollen and footprints."

"We'll need some dental stone, if you got it," said T.

"Never leave home without it," said Joel. "Got a twenty-five-pound box sitting in the van. Got large Ziploc baggies too."

"My, aren't you the resourceful one. My kind of guy," said T.

Joel smiled and led the way to the van.

Jay Dee mixed up the dental stone—two parts powder and one part water—in the gallon Ziploc bag. He wanted the consistency of pancake batter so he could pour it into the footprints without having to build a dam around the prints.

T used his new druggist fold to collect pollen samples from one of the bushes on the right side of the footprint and used Jay Dee's druggist fold for the bush on the left side.

"How long before those are ready?" asked T.

"About thirty minutes," said Jay Dee. "I mixed it pretty thick, so it shouldn't take that long to harden.

"Cool," said T. "I'll take one more look around and see if we missed anything."

Jay Dee stayed with the footprints, and as it started to harden, he used a stick to etch his initials and date in the topside of the drying dental stone. Once completely hardened, Jay Dee dug out underneath on one side of the footprint. He and T used their fingers to gently lift the casted footprint from the ground.

"Looks good, very good," said T.

"Yeah," said Jay Dee. "Still partly covered in mud, but we can clean that off once we get to the lab. Do you have your samples ready?"

"Yeah, right here." T patted his chest pocket. "Sealed tighter than Dick's hatband. I like that druggist fold."

Back at the lab, Jay Dee washed the remaining mud from the cast of the footprint, revealing treads that appeared to be from a Nike tennis shoe.

"Looks like a size 8, maybe 8 1/2," said T.

"Yeah," said Jay Dee. "Let's go check out our suspect's footwear."

"I need to get some tape and some three-foot-wide butcher paper, if you have any handy," said T to Joel.

"Yes, right over here. How much do you need?"

"Three feet by three feet," replied T. "And if you have the tape that dissolves in alcohol, I'll like a roll of that too."

"Yes, sir!" said Joel. "I've been waiting to use that tape but never really had a cause to do so."

"Now you do," said T.

All three headed down to the interrogation room, where the suspect was waiting. They were met outside the door of the interrogation room by Officer Lopez.

After introductions, T asked Officer Lopez if he was one of the officers who found the suspect.

"Yes," said Officer Lopez. "We spotted him sneaking around the rocks not far from the break-in. Says his name is Hector Zavala, but he has no ID."

"He has been read his rights?" asked Jay Dee.

"Yes," said Lopez, "and he waived them. Says he has nothing to hide. Says he was fishing and lost his rod and reel in the water. He was climbing up the rocks when we found him."

"Does he live nearby?" asked T.

"No," answered Lopez. "He lives in the cut. Said he rode his bike. We did find a bike hidden in some bushes not far from where we picked him up. Search of his person revealed this." Officer Lopez held up a clear plastic bag containing a large folded knife.

"Big knife," said T. "Five, five and a half inches? Kind of overkill for fishing, don't you think?"

"Agreed," said Lopez, "but that's his story."

"Thank you, Officer Lopez," said Jay Dee. "Can you sign that over to Joel, and let him begin matching it to some of the tool marks I've collected at the scene?"

Lopez nodded and handed Joel a pen. Joel signed the chain-of-custody marker on the bag and took the knife back to the lab.

"You let us know what you find out," said T.

"You'll know as soon as I do," said Joel.

87

Entering the interrogation room, Jay Dee and T saw a five-foot-six Hispanic male who appeared to be about twenty-eight years old. Both noticed right away he was wearing a pair of Nike tennis shoes.

"I'm Ranger Baker, and this is Ranger Jones. And you are?"

"My name is Hector Zavala. Oh, Texas Rangers, huh?"

"Have you been read your rights?" asked T.

"Yes," replied Hector. "I have nothing to hide."

"Great," said Jay Dee. "We'd like to ask you a few questions. What were you doing down by the rocks last night?"

"I already told those other dudes. I was fishing."

"You've not asked why you are being detained," said T.

Hector didn't say anything.

"Do you know why you are here?" asked Jay Dee.

"I thought it was for fishing without a license," Hector said, smiling.

"Not quite," said T. "There was a break-in at a house not far where you were found crawling across the rocks."

"A break-in, huh?" said Hector. "So you arrest the first Hispanic guy you see? Good thing I'm not black. I might not have made it back to the station."

T got up and unrolled the butcher paper onto the floor next to Hector. "Mr. Zavala, could you remove your shoes and stand on this butcher paper, please?"

"What for?" asked Hector.

"We just want to compare your shoes to some footprints we found at the crime scene," said Jay Dee.

"I don't think I want to do that," said Hector.

"Actually, you don't have a choice in this matter," said T.

"Either you can do it voluntarily, or Officer Jones will help you," said Jay Dee.

Hector stared at T for a good minute. "You think you're bad, big man. Okay, okay, I'll take off my shoes; no problem." Hector loosened the laces to his already untied tennis shoes and slipped them off his feet.

Jay Dee looked inside the tongue. "Size 8."

"So what?" said Hector. "It don't mean nothing."

"Stand on the paper," said T.

"Do this, do that, stand here. What the fuck do I want to stand on the paper for?"

"The sooner you do, the sooner you'll be done here," said Jay Dee.

Hector reluctantly stepped on the butcher paper.

T used a clean fingerprint brush he had taken from the crime scene lab and began whisking the brush up and down Hector's pants leg. He then took out the roll of tape Joel had given him, unrolled six-inch strips, and began sticking it to Hector's sleeves and the front and back of his shirt.

"You collecting lint?" asked Hector, as he stepped off the butcher paper.

After folding the butcher paper into a giant druggist fold, Jay Dee stood up. "We just collected pollen samples from your clothing. We are going to have these compared to some we took from the crime scene."

"You've heard of DNA, right?" asked T.

"Yes," said Hector. "What does that have to do with pollen?"

"Just like people," said T, "plants have their own unique DNA."

"Bullshit!" said Hector.

"No, he is right," said Jay Dee. "If they had used it in the Simpson case, OJ would have been convicted."

"I'm hungry," said Hector.

"We'll get you something; just sit tight," said T. He and Jay Dee exited the room.

Outside, Officer Lopez held up a plastic bag in each hand for Jay Dee and T to see. One contained a prophylactic, still in its original package. The other contained a black ski mask with orange stripes. "Officers found these floating in the bay near where we picked this guy up."

"We need to take the wet mask out of the plastic, and let it air dry," said Jay Dee.

"Any prints on the packaging of the condom?" asked T.

"No," said Officer Lopez. "They were in the water. Figured all prints would be washed away."

"Not necessarily," said T. "We can try SPR."

"SPR?" asked Lopez.

"Small particle reagent," said T. "Chemicals you mix and spray on evidence that's been submerged in water. Sometimes you get chicken, and sometimes you get feathers."

Lopez looked at T quizzically.

"What my colleague here means is that sometimes it works, sometimes it doesn't," said Jay Dee. "Has this guy been fingerprinted yet?"

"No," said Lopez. "We are just holding him. Don't have enough to arrest him yet."

Jay Dee held up the tennis shoe. "Maybe these will change that. We will know soon enough. Get him a taco and some coffee. We're headed to the lab."

88

"Looks like a match to me," said T. "You see that missing tread near the heel?"

"Yeah, kinda like he was dragging his feet," said Jay Dee.

"Right. It's missing on the shoes and the prints we collected from the crime scene."

"Not enough to convict," said Jay Dee, "but enough to get fingerprints from this guy. Why don't you work on the packaging of the condom."

T turned to Joel. "Got any SPR?"

"Sure do," said Joel. "Used it last week to take prints off a car we found dumped in the back bay."

"Did it work?" asked T.

"Like a charm," said Joel.

"Good," said T. "Let's mix up another batch and see if we can pull anything off this condom wrapper."

"Easy enough." Joel took the wrapper and headed toward the fume hood. "Strong stuff; don't want to inhale this."

T looked on as Joel mixed the powder into the liquid solution and inserted a pump spray lid onto the container. Using nitrile gloves, Joel removed the condom wrapper from the evidence bag and attached it to a small alligator clip hanging from a wire suspended across the inside of the chemical hood. Joel then proceeded to spray both sides with the SPR. Almost immediately, two fingerprints appeared, one on each side of the wrapper.

"Damn," said T. "Those are pretty! You do good work."

"We do our best," said Joel modestly.

"What are you two guys smiling about?" asked Jay Dee.

T and Joel moved away to allow Jay Dee a clear view of the prints on the wrapper.

"My, my," he said. "Isn't science wonderful? Let's go see if Hector has finished his taco. Don't want our boy having to eat with inked fingers."

89

Kat sat on the back porch with her dad, having an after-dinner drink—he with his usual Pacifico, and Kat with a tall glass of her mom's sweet iced tea. She felt vibrations from her phone ringing, slid it out, and saw it was Jay Dee calling. As tempted as she was to take the call, she silenced her phone.

"Work?" her dad asked.

"Sí," said Kat.

"Important?"

"I'll find out tomorrow."

"I'm very proud of you, my dear. You made your way in a man's world. Are you going to make me wait all night and tell me in the morning?"

"Tell you what?" asked Kat.

"Why you are here."

"I can handle my own, most of the time. But every now and then, I just need to get away. You help me stay centered. You always have. You are my rock. The one I go to when I can't go to anyone else."

"Your mother and I are always here for you, mija."

"I know. I know I can talk to you. I have a lot on my plate at the moment. I can't really say what. I just need some time for things to work themselves out. That's all."

"Okay. Understood."

Her mom came through the back door and handed her dad another beer.

"More tea, mija?" she asked.

"No, thank you. I'm fine," said Kat.

"Seeing anybody?" asked her mom.

"I don't know. Maybe," Kat said.

"What does that mean?" asked her mom.

"There is someone," said Kat. "We haven't gone out yet, but I think that is about to change."

"Someone from work?" her dad asked.

"Sí," said Kat.

"Was that him who called earlier?" asked her dad.

"Sí," said Kat.

"So why are you wasting time talking to an old man when you can be talking to a young man?"

"I'll talk to him tomorrow, Daddy. Tonight I just want to watch the fireflies and visit with you and Mama."

Kat spent the rest of the evening talking about everything except work and the new flame that recently had been lit.

90

Kat slept late the following morning.

"No need to rush back until I get the DNA results," she told her father over coffee as her mother made migas.

"That is what's been troubling you, mija?"

"Yes, you recall we lost two detectives?"

"Of course," said her mother. "You've been so busy with work since then that we never get to see you."

"I know, Mama, but I've been overloaded with the investigation of Captain Moore's wife, and now I'm looking into the loss of my fellow officers too."

"I thought I read in the papers that the captain's wife died in an accidental drowning."

"You did, Papa. That was just for the papers. Can't really talk about it right now, though."

"It's difficult to go north, mija, when being pulled south, east, and west," said her dad. "You must focus on the most pressing issue, and go that way first. Once that task is complete, you will have more time and energy to focus on the next one."

"Kind of like how you advised me to pay off my credit cards, huh, Dad?" asked Kat.

"Exactly. Your mama and I own this house outright. We have no car payment. We pay cash for our groceries, and when we do use a card, we pay it off each month. But it wasn't always like that, raising five children. We developed a plan of attack and got ourselves out from under that burden of debt. You can do the same."

"If only it were that easy," replied Kat.

"Easy," her mom began. "You think it was easy buying groceries for four boys and you? You ate almost as much as they did. I shopped at the thrift stores and garage sales in Corpus to buy school clothes so no one would recognize the clothing you children wore. Easy? No vacations. Your dad was working two jobs so that I could cook every meal. We aren't saying it will be easy, mija. But your father has provided well for our family, and he has given you good advice. We raised you to be smart enough to follow it. Now go and do so, as much as I hate to see you leave. We both love you so much, but you must end the turmoil inside before it ruins you."

Kat stood and hugged her mother and father. "Thank you," she said. "Thank you for being wonderful parents. I know you worked hard for us. I can't tell you how much I love you both. I want you to be proud of my accomplishments."

"We are, mija," said her father. "We love you very much—always have, always will."

91

Kat took her time on her drive back to her apartment in Corpus Christi. The forty-five minutes gave her an opportunity to formulate a plan of attack. "First, I'll deal with the chief about Aguilar," Kat said aloud, which she often did while formulating her thoughts. "I just need the DNA results from the shirt. Next, I'll see where the DA stands on Captain Moore's case. Then, I'll check on the Rangers and see what they've been working on. Finally, I'll find out if Jay Dee feels the same connection as I do. Every cell in my body is telling me he does."

Her conversation with herself was rudely interrupted by her cell phone. She recognized the number and pushed the hands-free button. "Hola, Joel. Tell me—what did the lab come up with?"

"I'm not sure if this is good news or bad news," said Joel. "The blood on the shirt we took from Detective Aguilar's trash matches Timms's and Huerta's. My supervisor just called Chief Gibson. I thought I would give you the heads-up."

"Appreciate that Joel. I'll be back later this afternoon. I'm gonna let this stew for a bit. You did good work, Joel, as always. Thank you."

When Kat reached her apartment, she showered, dressed, and fixed a late lunch, but she was unable to eat. "One at a time," she told herself as she left her apartment.

Kat went straight to see Chief Gibson.

"He's not there," said Juanita. "He and Captain Moore went down to see Detective Aguilar."

"Thank you so much for one at a time," said Kat as she left the room.

Jay Dee and T were at their desks when Kat walked in.

T rose to great her. "There she is."

"Good afternoon," said Jay Dee. "Glad you're back."

"I've heard bits and pieces about the rapist we've been after," said Kat. "Looks like you two have been taking names and kicking butts. I want to hear all the details, once we blow this Popsicle stand. Got some business to attend to first. See you in a few."

The chief was sitting behind Captain Moore's desk when Kat entered the room. Captain Moore was seated in a chair across the room; Javier was standing in front of the chief, using his hands in animated gestures.

"Did I interrupt something?" asked Kat.

"Come in," said the chief. "Detective Aguilar was just explaining how Timms's and Huerta's blood were found on one of his shirts. You came in at just the right time. It seems that Javier thinks you may have had something to do with that. What do you have to say?"

"I say that it's idiotic to claim that Timms and Huerta shot each other," said Kat. "The evidence clearly points to the shooter being in the back seat. Also, the shooter would have blood on himself as well as on any clothing he was wearing. The vehicle was then conveniently sent into the Gulf, washing away any trace evidence. Detective Aguilar claims he entered the water to check on the passengers in the vehicle. He could then have replaced his blood-stained shirt with a fresh one—everyone knows he keeps a fresh shirt in the trunk of his cruiser so his wife won't smell perfume from the girls at the strip joint that he likes to frequent. He also claims that shots were fired from the dunes and that he returned fire, explaining why he had traces of GSR on his hands. I have to admit that's a good plan, but there's no evidence of a shooter being in the dunes. Did I spell it out clearly enough for you gentlemen?"

All three men looked at Kat without saying a word.

Captain Moore finally stood and broke the silence. "I've had about all of this I can take. I'll discuss our other matter later, Chief. Looks like you've got your hands full with this one. Wish I could help, but I still have no official capacity here." Captain Moore shook Chief Gibson's hand before exiting the room.

Once outside, Captain Moore saw the two Rangers sitting at their desks. "I'm Captain Moore."

The two rose to shake Moore's hand. "I'm Jay Dee Baker, and this Terrance Jones, Texas Rangers, sir. Pleased to meet you."

"I've heard nothing but good things about you two. Bet you can't wait to get back to the Rangers. Thanks for helping us out. You two have a job here, if either of you decides to stay."

"Appreciate that," said T. "Corpus is starting to grow on me a bit. Not the wind, mind you, but the water is pretty."

"Well, think about it. Looks like we're going to have another vacancy soon." Moore then turned and walked out the door.

Minutes later, Kat exited Moore's office, smiling. "Excellent work, you two. Let's celebrate. I'm buying."

"Thanks, but Carolynn is in town, so I'll have to take a rain check," said T.

Kat looked at Jay Dee.

"I'm in," he said. "Where to?"

"I know just the place. And no rain check for you," she said, pointing to T.

Kat drove, and Jay Dee followed, to a little bar she liked to frequent. After a couple of pints of Dos Equis, Jay Dee excused himself and slid from the bar stool. When he returned, he could tell Kat was not welcoming the advances from the behemoth now sitting on his bar stool.

"Mind if I have my chair back?" Jay Dee said, standing between Kat and the stranger.

"Fuck off."

"I don't want any trouble with you, sir, but I was sitting there before you, so if you don't mind, I'd like my seat back." Jay Dee held his ground, even though the stranger towered over him.

Kat realized that things were beginning to escalate and that this stranger outweighed Jay Dee by close to a hundred pounds. She tried to leave, pulling Jay Dee with her.

"Pussy!" yelled the stranger.

Turning back to face the giant, Jay Dee smiled. "You are what you eat." He paused for effect and then continued. "Tell me—how does *asshole* taste?"

The stranger threw a punch with his right hand. Jay Dee saw the roundhouse coming and easily ducked under it. He then punched the abdomen of his attacker, causing him to lean forward at the waist, gasping for air. Jay Dee finished the job with a left uppercut to the chin, rendering the man unconscious.

Kat checked the guy for a pulse as Jay Dee stood over him.

"He's breathing," she said. "Let's get the hell out of here."

"Fine by me. My beer was getting warm anyway."

Kat grinned. "I know where we can get some cold beer. I'll drive. You've got a lot of balls, taking on that giant."

"Just two is all," said Jay Dee as he slid into the passenger side, with Kat quickly putting the Mustang in gear.

"Well, they must be big," said Kat, looking straight at Jay Dee.

Jay Dee laughed. "I hear that quite often."

Minutes later, they pulled into a small town house parking lot. It didn't take a detective for Jay Dee to figure out they were entering Kat's apartment. She tossed the keys on a stand by the door. "Beer's in the fridge. I'm gonna jump into the shower. Help yourself." She disappeared down the hallway.

Jay Dee popped the top on a beer and took a swig. He didn't need a shot of courage—good sense, maybe, but not courage. He carried the beer down the hall.

The sound of running water drew him through a bedroom and to the half-open door leading to the master bath.

"Room in there for two?" Jay Dee asked while undressing.

"I was wondering." Kat opened the curtain. "That for me?" Jay Dee handed Kat the bottle. "I wasn't talking about the beer," she said as she grabbed his erection.

Jay Dee pressed his naked body against hers and kissed Kat deeply. He then maneuvered his right thigh in between her legs, lifting slightly to put pressure on her clitoris. Kat moaned, leaned her head back, and began rocking her hips, grinding against his thigh.

Jay Dee used his femur as a means of sexual exploration. Kat's eyes were closed, her breathing was rapid, and her moans were getting louder.

"Fuck me, fuck me, fuck me," Kat said as she came—once, then again and again.

Jay Dee moved slightly to the right, now using his rock-hard erection to cause her to come again. He then slid his hands from the top of each side of her hips to the underside of Kat's ass and, raising her up to him, kissed her hard on the mouth, tongues intertwined.

Kat, now straddling him, flung her arms in ecstasy, knocking the shower curtain to the floor. Water went everywhere, but Kat laughed and thought, *It's just water.*

Jay Dee released his grip on her ass to turn the water off. Kat took his hand and led him to her bedroom, both dripping wet. She pushed him down onto her full-size bed and then sat on top of the still-solid shaft pointing toward the ceiling.

"Un momento," Kat said as she reached over to a drawer in the nightstand by her bed and pulled out a small packet containing a rubber. Tearing off the top of the packaging, she laughed and said, "Safety first."

Kat placed the condom in her mouth. Scooting backward, she took Jay Dee into her mouth. Now it was his turn to moan. His groin rose to meet Kat's offering.

Minutes later, Jay Dee reached down and pulled Kat up toward him, positioning her pussy slightly atop his cock, making entry smooth and quick. She felt so good and warm; Jay Dee wanted to release but held off.

Kat, now atop Jay Dee, began lifting her hips to expose a portion of his penis, being sure to keep the head still inside her, then slamming her soaking-wet pussy to swallow up the rest of his dick—slowly at first and then faster and faster until they both came.

Kat rolled off to lie beside Jay Dee. Her head rested atop his arm. "I'm not going to find a chewed-off arm in the morning, am I?" she asked, laughing.

"No way, baby, that was perfuck. You are incredible." Jay Dee kissed her on the lips.

"Good, 'cause you would have to walk back to your car. I drove, remember, and I'm not getting out of this bed before noon. Perfuck, huh. I like that."

"You know I really like sunrise sex," said Jay Dee.

"Never tried it, but like T says, first man to eat a coconut took a chance. Get some sleep, and if something pops up, just poke me." Kat kissed Jay Dee good night as if they had been lovers for life. *Who knows? Maybe we will be,* she thought. *Perfuck.*

The following morning Kat could hear a man's voice coming from her kitchen. She reached over and felt the bed. Jay Dee was missing. She arose, put on a T-shirt and panties, and covered herself with a robe.

Alarm came over her as Kat now made out what he was saying—or reading, as she recognized her written words.

"Oh my God," Jay Dee said. "Not only did she frame Captain Moore, but she killed those two detectives and framed Aguilar for it."

Kat ran into the kitchen. "What the fuck?" she yelled, pissed as hell.

"'What the fuck' is right," said Jay Dee. "I'm stunned."

"You go snooping through the stuff of every woman you fuck while she sleeps?"

"Some words caught my eye as you reached for the condom. I saw my name. This was open in the drawer."

"So that gives you the right to just help yourself to my things? That's mine; give it back." She reached for the notebook in Jay Dee's hands.

"Not so fast." He jerked the notebook away from Kat's grasp. "Talking about the right. I should be reading you your rights. This is sick stuff. You killed bums to increase the homicide rate, just so you could make detective. Then you set up some 'Skid Row Killer' to take the fall. This diary is evidence."

"Bullshit!" yelled Kat. "That's no diary."

"What the hell is it, then? A recipe for murder?"

Kat pulled open a kitchen drawer and drew out a pistol. "Those are notes for my novel." Her tone became sarcastic. "You think I'm the kind of person who writes a diary? Give me a fuckin' break. You've heard that fact is better than fiction. With all that's happening around here, you can't make that shit up. I just tweaked it a bit to spice things up—you know, give it a twist. And as for your name, you can just forget that. As of right now, you no longer grace the pages of my book. That's a shame. You were a great lay too. Guess I'll have to make do." Taking the notebook from Jay Dee, she said, "You can leave now."

Stunned, Jay Dee picked up his phone from the kitchen table and walked out the front door without saying a word.

Once outside, Jay Dee spoke into his phone. "You hear all that, T?"

"Yeah, I did. She pull a gun?"

"Fuckin' A, buddy. Hey, I need a ride."

"Sounds like you've been taken on one already. You think she did all those things you read, or is she really writing a novel?"

All Jay Dee could say was, "Damned if I know."

CPSIA information can be obtained
at www.ICGtesting.com
Printed in the USA
LVHW110500260319
611853LV00001B/63/P